Death Undercover

A 1920s historical mystery

A Dora and Rex Mystery
Book 3

Lynn Morrison

Marketing Chair Press

Cover design by DLR Cover Designs

Published by

The Marketing Chair Press, Oxford, England

LynnMorrisonWriter.com

Print ISBN: 978-1-7392632-3-2

Contents

1. Dora packs her case   1
2. A room with a view   10
3. A full house   17
4. The gruesome discovery   28
5. Too many surprises   35
6. Rex stands in the spotlight   43
7. Inga to the rescue   51
8. Benedict stands his ground   58
9. Playing the role of Constable   66
10. Police browbeating   74
11. Dora pulls back the curtain   81
12. Rex makes inquiries   92
13. The guessing game   100
14. Another unexpected arrival   108
15. That time in Ireland   115
16. News from the rumour mill   124
17. Dora goes undercover   131
18. A ghastly confession   139
19. Dora plays croquet   148
20. The roaster   156
21. The trap snaps shut   163
22. The grind of justice   171
23. A final toast   179
24. The big reveal   188
25. A heart to heart   197
26. The partnership is official   207
    Bonus Epilogue   215
    Historical Notes   221
    Double Cross Dead   223

Acknowledgments   225
About the Author   227
Also by Lynn Morrison   229

In loving memory of Kenzie, Emma, and the other children we lost far too soon.

Chapter 1
Dora packs her case

Theodora Laurent sat on the floor in the middle of her Belgravia bedroom, cushioned by the thick Persian carpet. The crackling flames in the nearby fireplace warmed the back of her silk pyjamas. Red velvet curtains, still closed against the weak morning sun, dampened the outside noise until all she heard was the ticking of the antique clock on the mantle and the periodic crack of the firewood. The only light in the room came from the pair of lamps on either side of the bed.

Dora sat with her legs crossed in a lotus shape and her hands resting on her knees. She'd learned this pose from an Indian yogi she'd met on her travels through the British empire. He'd promised her that taking a few minutes every day to quiet her mind would work wonders on her fortitude and grant her inner peace.

Dora made a point of undertaking a moment of silent meditation before setting off on any of her assignments. This one was particularly thorny, even if she had volunteered for it. In the coming days, her goal was to finally get proof that Count Vasile Zugravescu was a foreign spy.

The first time she'd met him, she'd been a newly minted

1

British spy with a code name and cover story... and her innocence. Her training had included everything except how to defend herself against her serious feelings of attraction. Count Vasile's smouldering dark looks and deluge of compliments had lit her heart on fire. In the wake of the Great War, far from almost everyone she knew, she was powerless against the desires he inflamed.

She'd dropped her guard and nearly lost her life in the process. If she hadn't stumbled across his plot to capture a British spy before he realised that spy was her, she'd be sitting now in some foreign prison.

Worst of all, it was pure, dumb luck she'd managed to get away. Not unscathed, however. She had a scar on her inner thigh and another on her heart to remind her of the price of blind love.

The next time their paths crossed, she'd looked at him with open eyes. In the fallow fields of her closed-off heart, she began having doubts about his dubious, if distant, claims to a foreign throne, and everything else he'd told her.

It was more likely that the name and title were a cover, just as Theodora Laurent was for her. But his employer and his actual history remained out of reach.

That infuriated her.

Again and again, they found themselves in the same place. Dora didn't dare let on to how much she knew. She danced cheek-to-cheek with him, barely keeping her balance as they walked along the knife's edge.

She transformed herself from an innocent young woman to a devious femme fatale. Yet she'd never caught him at a disadvantage. With no other choice, she'd done whatever was required to keep him from finding out her secrets.

Now the time had come for her to turn the tables. She'd uncover the answer to the question of his loyalties. Dora had arranged for the perfect set-up, offering to host him at a country house party. She'd have full control over the environment and every staff member on her payroll. Best of all, she'd have Rex, Inga, and the rest of her crack team with her.

It was a foolproof plan. She was positive it would go off without any issues.

And yet, she still suffered from a certain disquiet, all due to an unexpected gift.

Normally, the meditative practice delivered the results promised by the Indian yogi. With her palms facing upwards, ready to receive whatever the universe had in store for her, Dora had only to sit still, breathe deep, and listen.

Unfortunately, today, the universe had chosen to stick out its tongue at her request. She'd tried counting her breaths, pictured herself walking on a deserted path, and pretended to soar through the clouds. After a half hour of listening to the clock's infernal ticking, she'd resorted to conjugating irregular French verbs in her head.

Rather than getting closer, any hope of inner peace floated ever farther out of reach.

A knock on her bedroom door roused her from her reverie. "Stuff and nonsense," she muttered, groaning as her back twinged from sitting in one position for too long. She stood up. "Come in."

Her best friend and companion, Inga Kay, breezed through the doorway. She came to a sudden stop when her gaze landed on Dora. "You're still in your nightclothes? Rex is due to arrive in less than an hour and you haven't finished packing!"

"I'm nearly done," Dora countered, motioning toward the two giant travel chests sitting at the foot of the bed. "Cynthia did most of the work last night. I've only a few things to add. A quick change of clothes and I'll be ready."

"Hmm," was all Inga said in reply.

Dora hoped Inga would take the hint and leave her to get changed in peace, but the woman refused to budge. Instead, she wandered into Dora's dressing room to see for herself how much progress Dora had made.

"What is this?" Inga's voice echoed from the next room over. Dora froze in the alert pose of a deer hearing the first howls of the baying hounds. Mayhap if she didn't move, the danger would pass.

It was no use. Inga came to her.

Unlike Dora, Inga had dressed for a day of travelling in a simple wool dress in her favourite shade of dark red. She'd twisted her auburn hair into a tight coil to keep it from blowing in the wind during their drive. Inga held a hanger in her hand, with her arm lifted high enough to keep the pink fabric from dragging across the floor.

"Where in the world did this come from?" she asked.

Dora flicked her wrist at the empty box sitting on the desk.

Inga perked up at the sight of the white rectangular box. The telltale silver tissue paper peeking out from under the half-open lid proclaimed it to be from Dora's favourite couturière. Without a word, she laid the pink monstrosity of a gown across Dora's bed and dived into the box, looking for an explanation.

Inside, she found a thick, white card with a message penned in black ink. "From a fond admirer?" Inga spun around to gape at Dora. "That's it? Where's the rest of the message?"

"I think the dress is the rest of the message," Dora replied in a bone dry tone. She crossed the room to gaze upon the creation. "It arrived yesterday evening, while you and Harris were out."

The evening gown was cut in the latest fashion, sent over via special delivery from Paris. Made of pale pink satin, tiers of white chiffon decorated the skirt. The designer intended for it to hang loose enough to allow the owner to dance the night away.

Inga grimaced in distaste. "This isn't a dress. It's a wedding cake."

She wasn't wrong, even if Dora failed to be amused.

"Are you sure they didn't include it by mistake?"

Dora shook her head. "I sent Archie out with a telegram and told him not to leave the office until he got a reply. Monique confirmed. Someone ordered the dress via post and requested it be sent via courier. On the matter of who and why, she had no explanation."

"This may be the first time in my life I'm left speechless. This dress couldn't be less appropriate for you if it tried. If anything, the creation is better suited for an eighteen-year-old slip of a girl in her first season."

Dora didn't disagree with a word Inga said. She hadn't worn a dress that innocent since her earliest days as a spy, when she'd shed the last traces of her former life as Lady Dorothy.

Not since her initial encounter with Vasile.

It hadn't taken hours of contemplation for her to guess the identity of her so-called fond admirer. "I think Vasile sent this to me."

"Vasile?" Inga's head whipped around and she stared agog.

Dora gave a slow nod of confirmation. "He's reminding me of how we first met. How young I was. He's teasing me for settling down. The implied message is obvious. Theodora Laurent, society vixen, is now once again a tamed, clawless kitten."

Inga scrunched her brow and pondered Dora's words. "But he hasn't seen you in almost a year. How could he possibly think that? Not that I'm in any way suggesting it's true," she rushed to add.

Dora flicked the pink fabric, folding the gown over so she didn't have to look at its full glory. Even then, it continued to taunt her. She turned her back on it and flopped into the nearest chair to gaze up at the ceiling. "I'm in a quandary."

Inga strode over and stood directly behind Dora's chair, leaning over so she forced Dora to look her in the eye. In a tone drier than the Sahara, she said, "You don't say."

Her deadpan delivery caused Dora to snort with laughter. She straightened up and waved to the nearby chair. "Sit down for a moment so we can discuss this like civilised people."

Inga took the proffered seat and helped herself to the now lukewarm tea. She lifted the ceramic teacup to her mouth, taking care to keep her pinky finger sticking out. "My lady, my time is yours." She punctuated her statement by taking a sip of the tea.

Her resulting expression of disgust had Dora laughing again. "I'm at a crossroads, Inga, and I don't know what to do with myself."

"I know we've tarried in England longer than you originally anticipated, but there's nothing holding us here. Is there?" Inga wagged her eyebrows.

"You're actually going to make me say the words?"

Inga nodded.

"Fine," Dora huffed. "I find Rex to be... intriguing."

"Is that how you young people call it today? It's only us hens here, so you might as well come right out and say it. You fancy Rex. I'm fairly certain he also fancies you. And that's fine. Go ahead, indulge. You'll be better once you get it out of your system. I'm hardly one to judge anyone's choice of partner. But that doesn't explain why you are letting Vasile's jest get to you."

"Because I've let my affection for Rex cause me to take my eye off the ball. We haven't stayed in one location this long since we left the war front. As for missions, even those are hardly our usual challenge." Dora sniffed. "I'm supposed to be England's greatest secret spy, and here I am cooling my heels in a Belgravia townhouse... by choice. By choice!" she huffed. "Maybe I should wear that pink dress."

"Over my dead body..." Inga mumbled into her teacup. She glanced up to see Dora picking at her fingernail. It was time for an intervention. "Oh, do stop with the histrionics, Dora. So what that you've left the field, albeit temporarily? If Vasile thinks that means you're domesticated, then he's more addled than you are."

Dora removed the offending ragged fingernail from her mouth. She tilted her head enough to meet Inga's gaze. "Go on..."

Inga set her cup on the saucer and did as ordered. "Only someone who is a true master, who understands every aspect of their craft, can teach their skills to someone else. You've hardly sat around eating bonbons. Every single day you've got up and matched wits with Rex. Yes, he posed little challenge to start, but you can't deny his progress. You've studied, practiced, modelled, and tested yourself again and again. Personally, I can't wait until you have the last laugh."

Dora opened her mouth to rebut, but found herself with nothing to say. Of course, the woman was right! Dora gave herself a mental slap upside the head for not seeing the truth on her own.

But Inga wasn't done.

"All that said, there is another critical point I want you to take to heart."

Inga's tone was so serious that Dora shifted position until she was sitting up straight. "I'm listening."

Inga leaned forward and gathered Dora's hands in her own. "There is a universe of difference between soft and weak. Does the soft fur pelt of a lioness lessen the power of her bite? Does my love for Harris diminish my value to you? Throughout history, men have mistaken a woman's gentle affection for weakness. Yet, there is no greater fury than a woman aggrieved. Don't believe me? Try taking a babe from a mother's arms. Even the Bible says hell's power pales in comparison."

The mantle clock chimed the half hour. Inga let their hands drop and stood to dispel the serious mood. "Time waits for no woman, and neither will our ride. Bring the dress and hang it where you will see it every time you enter your room. Let it serve as a reminder."

"Of my strength?"

Inga had her hand on the bedroom door. She glanced at Dora over her shoulder. "No, my friend. It is testament to Vasile's blind confidence. Mark my words — this trip will spell the end of his career."

Having said her piece, Inga left the room to track down the housemaid.

Dora sauntered into her dressing room. She scanned the contents of her wardrobe until she spotted the item she wanted.

Made of jet black lace, the front of the floor-length gown was decorated with gleaming beads and swirls of sequins. The neckline dipped low enough to raise eyebrows, while the cinched waist highlighted the wearer's slender physique. Only a thin lining protected the wearer's modesty. It was a gown for a queen of the night — a woman daring enough to walk the tightrope between flawless and fatally beautiful.

Dora pulled the dress from the rack and set it aside for Cynthia to pack. This was a gown meant for Theodora Laurent.

She'd wear the gown with pride. She'd show Vasile she was no tamed beast and instead was every bit as strong and determined as he remembered.

And if Rex tossed an extra glance her way, all the better. She'd finally best Vasile and then clear her schedule for a nice, long week or two with Rex. Far away from danger, she'd scratch that particular itch and then return to the field. Rex would be fully trained and ready to go his own way.

Her dilemma resolved, Dora raised her hands up to her chest and pressed her palms together. She closed her eyes, took a deep breath, and then released it with a long, cleansing sigh.

It turned out that the universe had an answer for her, after all.

Chapter 2
A room with a view

Rex turned his back on the window in time to thank the footman after he set Rex's last travelling case in the bedroom. Ducklington's butler stood watch from the doorway, making sure his young charge put everything in its place.

After the footman left, exiting as silently as he'd arrived, the butler asked, "Do you require anything else, my lord?"

Rex surveyed his room, noting the plate of biscuits and pot of tea on the nearby end table. His valet would be up shortly to oversee the unpacking. "No, Percival. As always, you've seen to everything. The only thing I desire at this point is a few moments of quiet to reacquaint myself with my surroundings."

At that, the butler broke character long enough to show a rare smile. "After all your years of visiting Ducklington Manor, I find it hard to believe you've forgotten anything about it. That said, I'll leave you to your peace. Drinks will be served in the drawing room at eight."

Percival left the room, taking care to close the door quietly. Rex availed himself of the facilities to wash off the dust from their drive over. Once clean, he returned to his favourite place in the bedroom. It was the window nearest the bed, offering a southerly view of the house grounds.

Ducklington Manor took its name from the nearby Cotswold village of Ducklington. Located two miles to the west of the town square, the manor boasted extensive grounds and a forest full of deer and rabbits. The only reason Rex's father hadn't laid claim to the house was because it belonged to his grandmother. The Dowager Duchess of Rockingham purchased the house after her husband passed away and set to work, turning it into a place fit for a queen.

Nestled amongst the rolling hills, the house stood three floors high. The first change the dowager had enacted was the addition of a grandiose front hall and curving main staircase, perfect for making an entrance. Indeed, the twenty-room manor house had once played host to royalty, explaining the aptly named Queen Victoria and Prince Albert rooms.

Although the dowager had hosted many from the royal lines over the years, she'd always set aside a month in the summer for her grandchildren to visit. Instead of consigning Rex and his older brother to the upper floor nursery, she'd bidden them to make themselves at home. As long as they took care not to break anything valuable, she'd never once complained about their endless games of hide and seek.

The first time Rex came to Ducklington, he'd barely been tall enough to look over the window ledge in this bedroom. Gradually, he grew enough to expand his view. First, he set eyes on the gardens nearest the house. Behind them stood the stables and the green pens where the horses grazed. Further off in the distance, at the base of the next hill, sat the private lake.

As a grown man, he could survey the lake from shore to shore. The deep blue waters, gently lapping in the afternoon breeze, were home to fish, ducks, and one sea monster, or at least that was what his older brother had claimed. The threat of being eaten had never bothered Rex. If anything, he'd delighted in tempting fate by veering close to the water's edge. As a precocious youth, he'd been desperate to test his luck with a fishing rod, like the village boys he'd spotted playing from the carriage window.

His grandmother said the head groundskeeper could take Rex fishing when he was tall enough to spot the lake from his bedroom window. Thus, every time Rex visited, the window was his first port of call.

The head groundskeeper held true to his word. He'd arranged for some of the village boys to join in the fun. Rex finished the day sunburned, sore-armed, and thrilled with his newfound friends. The fish fry-up at the end of the day cemented his connection with the local lads. After that, Rex roamed the estate grounds with them every chance that he got. That was all thanks to his grandmother, who was determined to offer her grandsons a taste of normal life before their parents sent them to Eton to become men.

It took all of Rex's fortitude to squash the desire to saddle a horse and ride for the village, just like the old days. For now, he had other business to keep him occupied. But, with careful planning, he was almost certain he could fit in a pub night with his old mates before he had to return to London.

Perhaps he'd even bring Dora along with him. He chuckled out loud while he pictured the expressions on the villagers' faces.

Speaking of Dora, it was time to see how she was getting on. Rex circled the four-poster bed and approached the blank space of the wall between the nightstand and the wardrobe. It took him a moment to remember which etching in the wooden panelling hid the latch from sight. He twisted the near-invisible button and, after a muffled click, the panel swung open to reveal the outline of a tall, narrow doorway.

Behind the door ran a cramped corridor, barely wider than Rex's shoulders. He backtracked long enough to get a torch from the drawer in the nightstand. The beam of light illuminated a plain wooden floor swept clean of all dirt. Despite the hidden location, his grandmother instructed the servants to keep it spotless. After all, what good was a spy hallway if going into it made you sneeze?

He'd heard Percival instruct the footman to take Dora's things to the Delphinium bedroom, conveniently located only a few doors down from his own. The distance was even shorter if one knew of the existence of the secret passageways hidden behind the walls. Rex made a right turn and tread lightly until he spotted the hand-painted drawing of the tall, spiked purple blooms which gave the room its name.

A true gentleman would knock and request permission to enter a lady's boudoir. Rex, however, was looking forward to getting a jump on his almost preternaturally gifted mentor. He flipped the catch and pushed the door open in a single, smooth motion.

Dora barely looked up from the book she was reading. Rex recognised it as the one he'd packed for himself. When had she lifted it from his bag?

Dora, in her velvet chair near the fire, didn't seem surprised by his entrance or troubled by her blatant thievery. "I was wondering how long it would take you to come check on me. I'd have searched for you, but I wasn't sure which way to turn."

Rex switched his torch off and crossed his arms, scowling at the woman before him. "Stop bluffing and admit that I caught you off-guard. There's no way you heard me coming, nor knew about the existence of this door."

Dora raised her eyebrows. "Is that so? Come inside and we'll discuss this theory of yours."

Rex strode into the bedroom, pausing long enough to close

and secure the door. He waited for Dora to join him, but she motioned for him to stand beside her.

"I will confess to having a slight advantage, since you'd made me aware of the existence of the corridors and spy holes before we arrived. As soon as the footman left the room, I set to work exploring my space." Dora pointed to the left of the doorway through which Rex had arrived. "At first, I thought that Impressionist painting hid the access point, but it hangs by a single nail. If someone entered in a hurry, they'd run the risk of knocking it down. Once I was that close to the wall, I noticed a tiny gap between the seams of the wallpaper. It took little searching to locate the latch, even if the buds of the floral wallpaper brilliantly disguised it. Are you satisfied now or do I need to stand up and show you where it is?"

Rex huffed in frustration. The corners of his mouth turned into a pout he hadn't used since he was small. The childish expression caused Dora to laugh again.

"Poor, dear Rex! I can see I've ruined the surprise you had planned. How can I make it up to you? Shall I promise to delay searching for the hidden staircases until you give me the okay?"

Rex shook his head at Dora's tone. It sounded apologetic, but the sparkle in her eyes betrayed the lie. She wasn't sorry in the least. He reached down and tweaked her nose. "Minx! You may have bested me this time, but I daresay I have the advantage here. Uncovering all the secret hideaways will take a concerted effort. As a wise woman once told me, why reinvent the wheel when you can borrow one from a friend?"

Dora barked a laugh. "I did say that, didn't I? Well played, Rex. My time is yours, old chap. What would you like to show me first?" She rubbed her hands together and gave Rex a cheeky wink. "Shall we try to catch Inga off-guard?"

"She's on the other side of the hallway, I'm afraid. We'd have to pass in front of her door to reach the access point."

"Good to know! In that case, let's start with the guest-view of the house first. Show me all the bedrooms so we can decide who will be in each one. From there, we can delve into the specifics of how we can monitor our guests' movements without letting on."

Rex nodded his approval of her approach. "Right. I'll retrace my steps to my bedroom and meet you outside in the hall. It wouldn't do for the servants to spot me sneaking out of your quarters so early in the day. Such things are barely acceptable when done under the cover of darkness."

Dora rose from her chair and turned to stand nearly nose-to-nose with Rex. She raised her hand and traced her fingers down the front of his shirt. "Promises, promises!"

She spun away before Rex could gather his wits and picked up the book from the chair. "Daylight's burning. I'd like to size up the immediate house grounds before Percival sounds the gong for dinner. Give me five minutes to get changed and then I'm yours."

Dora handed him his book and shooed him out of the hidden doorway. Despite his short-term failings, Rex arrived back at his starting point in good humour.

No, he hadn't managed to one-up Dora. Not yet, anyway. But he wasn't without hope.

Unlike their previous missions, he'd signed on to this one with no arm-twisting required. Ducklington Manor was his childhood habitat. He knew every servant by name and called a fair few men in the village his friends.

This was his moment in time to prove to Dora he was qualified to be her knight in shining armour. Not that she ever needed saving, but he had to believe for himself that he was up to the task. Only then would he allow himself to contemplate the meaning behind Dora's habit of giving him light touches and seductive glances.

He'd nearly convinced himself there was nothing to them. That all changed the moment she suggested she accompany him to the countryside. The Cotswolds were the last place one would find Theodora Laurent. She'd made her preference for city life clear, time and time again.

But on the heels of their last escapade, Lord Audley declared Rex had to absent himself. Faced with weeks without him, suddenly her tune had changed.

That act gave Rex hope that perhaps Dora's mother was right. But he didn't want a casual dalliance. For there to be something lasting between the two of them, Rex had to show he was worthy of the title of partner.

He intended to prove that to them both. All he had to do was survive a few days in the company of the foreign count, and use his resources to uncover the man's true identity. A little wining, dining, and spying, and that potential romance with Dora would be within reach.

He glanced down at the book in his hands. All those hours he'd spent studying the words of the Chinese general Sun Tzu had made an impact on Rex. As the text said, '*Plan for what is difficult while it is easy, do what is great while it is small.*'

Rex had every advantage in the world, and he intended to exploit them. If Sun Tzu were here, he'd no doubt congratulate Rex on his flawless plan. For the first time, Rex was convinced he couldn't fail.

Chapter 3
A full house

If there was one area in which Ducklington Manor fell short of Dora's wishes, it was in the choice of decor. The dowager duchess had invested in expensive furnishings when she bought the house in the later days of Victoria's reign. Although the trends moved on, the dowager's tastes did not.

The drawing room featured tall windows and a trio of Venetian crystal chandeliers. Despite ensuring an abundance of light both day and night, they did little to balance out the dark wood finish of the solid furniture and the deep maroon carpet.

The thick floor coverings and velvet upholstery of the settees muffled all noise. Ceramic vases, figurines, and heavy brass candlesticks took up space along the mantle, shelves, and tables. From the dour countenances on the family portraits to the harp sitting in the corner, everywhere she looked, Dora found another reminder to be on her best decorum.

Dora preferred open spaces with eclectic furniture, creating rooms where everyone felt free to be themselves. Ducklington Manor imposed just the opposite. At any other time, Dora would have risen to the challenge, proposing some outrageous parlour game or dragging in a gramophone. Today, unfortunately, such options remained absolutely out of the question.

The first of their weekend guests had arrived, and Dora and Rex had ensconced themselves in the drawing room with cups of tea in their hands. Across from them sat Lord and Lady Lambert, a more mismatched pair Dora had never seen.

Lord Lambert was a jolly, middle-aged man with pink cheeks, a bulbous nose, and a habit of chuckling after everything he said. His wife sat upright, without a hint of bend in her spine or her demeanour. Although she couldn't have been more than forty years of age, her clothing choice made her appear a decade older. Her staid, ankle-length skirt and high-necked blouse stood in stark contrast to Dora's wide-legged trousers and bright print sweater.

Ever since Rex had introduced Theodora as his companion, Lady Lambert had had her nose in the air and lips pursed as though she'd caught scent of a foul odour in the room.

That odour was, of course, Dora.

Her ladyship made it clear by her comportment that Dora was not her social equal, and therefore should not make any attempts to foster camaraderie. How this might work, given the intimate atmosphere of a country house party, was hardly her ladyship's concern.

Years of practice enabled Dora to maintain a smile throughout Lady Lambert's insults. Lord Lambert was either blithely unaware of, or else choosing to ignore, his wife's behaviour. He filled the gaps with a steady patter of conversation on plans for entertainment.

"Tell me, old boy, are we scheduled to hunt or fish tomorrow?"

"I believe clay shooting is in the cards, is it not?" Rex asked, turning to Dora. "Followed by a picnic, weather-permitting. At this time of year, we may need to retreat indoors."

"Let's hope it cooperates," said Lord Lambert, before casting an eye at his wife. "Remember the salmon mousse tartlets we had the last time we stayed here? They were your favourites, right, dear?"

"I doubt we'll have anything so refined without the dowager duchess here to oversee things." Lady Lambert said with a derisive sniff. "On that note, I'll excuse myself to oversee the unpacking. Goodness knows how the staff will behave."

Lord Lambert opted to once again remain oblivious to the barely veiled insults tumbling from his wife's mouth. He was all smiles as he thanked Rex for including them for the weekend and scuttled out on Lady Lambert's heels.

As soon as the door closed behind them, Dora slumped in her seat, tilted her face toward the ceiling, and huffed in frustration. "It's times like these that I'm half-tempted to reveal who I really am. If Lady Lambert knew she'd perched herself on the verge of offending the Viscountess of Lisle, I'm sure she'd sing a different song."

"Chin up," Rex said, reaching over to squeeze her arm. "This weekend is bound to change the fortunes of a few of our guests. Perhaps Lady Lambert will end up with mud on her face."

Dora contemplated the possibility and shook her head. "No, I'll never be so lucky."

* * *

A knock on the drawing-room door forced an end to that line of discussion. Ducklington's butler entered to announce another arrival. "Count Zugravescu is pulling into the drive," he intoned. "Shall I show him in?"

"Of course, Percival," Rex replied.

Dora studied Rex from the corner of her eye, checking whether he showed any signs of nerves. For the first time, he seemed completely at ease. Whether it was comfort knowing that he was king of this castle, or confidence borne from their days of planning, Dora couldn't say for sure.

She surprised even herself when she leaned over and kissed him on the cheek.

"What was that for... not that I'm complaining," Rex asked.

"For luck," she replied. But mostly out of genuine affection, not that she was ready to admit that. Not yet, anyway.

A few minutes later, the count strode into the drawing room, and with a dashing smile, transformed the staid atmosphere. Dora and Rex stood to greet him.

"Theodora!" Count Vasile exclaimed. His accent was as thick as always. Her name rolled off his tongue. He sauntered closer, his dark eyes flashing, and took the hand she offered. He executed a perfect bow as he bent over to kiss her knuckles. "You are absolutely radiant. A diamond of the first order. A star twinkling in the heavens..."

"Yes, yes," she said, cutting into his flow of compliments. "I see you haven't changed a bit, you naughty man."

Dora wasn't exaggerating. Vasile was as startlingly handsome as ever, with his bronzed skin, sharp cheekbones, firm chin, and dark looks. The double-breasted suit showed off his broad shoulders, while the tie and straw boater spoke of his European heritage.

Rex cleared his throat, and Dora rushed to complete the introductions. "Count Vasile, allow me to introduce you to Lord Rex, our host for the weekend."

The men locked hands in a firm handshake.

Dora's breath caught in her chest. That moment of connection was like seeing night meet day.

Once upon a time, Dora had yearned for the count's embrace. She'd let him wrap the shadows of night around her, protecting her from the memories of the funeral shrouds in the days following the Great War.

He'd seemed the embodiment of the devil himself. When he'd turned his gaze her way, she'd fallen head first, certain no other man would ever compare.

Certainly not a boring English boy from back home.

And yet, seeing them standing together, Dora couldn't tear her eyes off Rex. It wasn't just the months of running her fingers down his arms or giving spontaneous kisses that had her blood running hot.

Dora knew Rex — his doubts, fears, and dreams. That, more than his golden boy looks, gave him his appeal.

The count's falseness was evident in his every calculated move. From the way he squeezed Rex's hand in a silent challenge to his slow-eyed gaze as he scanned her from head to toe, nothing about his moves rang true. In the beginning, this had not bothered Dora. If anything, it only made her more intrigued.

That was because, before returning to England, she'd only had eyes for men like him. Men who promised a night and nothing more.

Now, however, she leaned in a new direction. She flipped her gaze between the two men and knew without question that this wasn't a competition. Not for her interest, anyway.

But now wasn't the time for bedroom fantasies. It was time for her to get to work. The count was here, and the game was afoot.

Count Vasile loosened his grip, and Rex pulled his hand free. Almost as one, the men shifted until Dora was at the centre of both their attention.

Unlike dealing with snooty, upper-class wives, this was a position where Dora thrived.

"My goodness! Where are our manners?" Dora resumed her position on the sofa, with Rex at her side, leaving Vasile to sit across from them. "Have a seat, Vasile, and tell us about your trip. When did you arrive in England?"

Vasile settled onto the settee with a slight groan as he relaxed against the cushioned back. "I arrived in Southampton at midnight. I intended to get some rest, but the hotel lost my reservation. Instead, I persevered for as long as I could keep my eyes open and made my way north."

Dora noted then the fine lines bracketing his mouth and the faint shadows under his eyes. He was telling the truth. "Where did you sleep?"

"Where else but in my car? It was horrible," he moaned in his thick accent. "When day finally broke and I made sense of the road signs, I drove to the nearest pub and availed myself of its rustic accommodations. After one of your famous breakfasts and a change of clothes, I felt somewhat more like myself."

"And then you had to get back into the car and drive here." Rex motioned to the tea. "You must be parched. Would you like a cup of tea or water, perhaps?"

"A finger of Scotch would be better," Count Vasile replied. "That should be enough to send me off to dreamland for a couple of hours of rest."

"Allow me," Dora said, rising before Rex could move. "I remember how you take your whiskey."

She swayed her hips while she walked over to the drinks cart, carefully positioning herself to block Vasile's view of the decanter. She selected a glass, tilted her hand to drop in one of Inga's infamous relaxation powders, and then topped it up with the requested amount of whiskey. Two cubes of ice, a splash of water, a quick swirl and it was ready. "Here you are, darling."

Dora segued into one topic after another until the count's glass was empty. When he lost the battle against a yawn, she leapt up and called for the butler. "Percival, would you mind showing Count Vasile upstairs? He'll be staying in the Hawthorn room."

The butler gave a stilted nod of confirmation. "Of course, madam. I've already had his things brought up. Right this way, my lord."

As soon as the door shut behind them, Rex spoke up. "Do you want me to ring for Inga so she can keep watch on him while we wait for the other guests?"

A sly smile spread across Dora's face. "He won't be going anywhere for the next few hours. In fact, we may even have to rouse him for dinner."

"I'm surprised you... err... encouraged him to rest."

"Keeping him awake might offer us a further advantage, but where would be the fun in that? It will be far more interesting to pit ourselves against him when we're all in fighting form."

Rex looked like he wanted to argue, but the sound of a motor car pulling up in front of the house put paid to that idea.

Dora hurried over to the window. "That will be the rest of them. Come on, we can meet them out front."

* * *

They made it to the front doorstep in time to see Rex's Rolls-Royce come to a stop. The remaining guests had travelled together on the train and Rex had sent the cars to collect them. Dora peered down the drive, but there was no sign of the second car.

The sound of a woman calling her name pulled her attention back to their newest arrivals — another couple from the guest list. At first, Dora thought her eyes were deceiving her, because the woman looked so much like herself.

Upon closer inspection, she noted that the woman's hair was a few shades darker, her wide-eyed gaze less calculating, and her mannerisms less smooth. That said, her choice of clothing was second to none. She wore a drop-waist dress in a subtle striped pattern, featuring a ruffled collar and long sleeves with buttoned cuffs. A fluffy fur coat and a pair of Mary Janes completed the ensemble.

The woman practically dashed over to meet Dora. "Miss Laurent, it's an honour to make your acquaintance. I've seen you in the society pages so often. I could hardly believe it when Elmer said you were to be our hostess."

"You must be Miss Dixon. You flatter me, and unnecessarily, I might add," Dora replied. While she shook the woman's hand, she switched her attention to the man following in Miss Dixon's wake.

This time, Rex beat her to the welcome. "Good afternoon, Sir Elmer, and welcome to Ducklington Manor. Please, allow me to introduce Miss Laurent."

Sir Elmer was a hulk of a man. His thick arm and leg muscles gave the seams of his wool coat and trousers a run for their money. The man reminded Dora of the lumberjacks in Grimm's tales. However, he had a warm smile and soft brown eyes that put her instantly at ease.

"Lord Rex, you're in fine form. As for Miss Laurent, the pleasure is mine." Sir Elmer paused long enough to shake Rex's hand. Then he lowered his voice and said to Dora, "Vasile has told me plenty of stories of his run-ins with you over the years. I can hardly wait to see what will happen when you're under the same roof. I'll be shocked if we get a wink of sleep with the two of you notorious night owls to keep us entertained."

Dora threw back her head and laughed. "Perhaps that's why the count opted to take an afternoon nap."

"So he's arrived?" Sir Elmer's smile widened. "That old devil. I'll take a page from his book and do the same. What say you, Ida?"

"I could prop my feet up for an hour before I get unpacked." Miss Dixon turned to Dora. "I didn't bring a lady's maid with me."

"It's no problem. I'll ask Mrs Johnson to arrange for a housemaid to lend you a hand. We're staying in the same wing of the house. In fact, I'm across the hall. The staff should have no trouble getting around to us all."

"That's mighty kind of you, Miss Laurent." Miss Dixon checked the time using a very expensive wristwatch. "Maybe in an hour or two? By then, I'll be right as rain."

A car horn echoed from the drive.

"That will be Mr and Mrs Murphy," Sir Elmer said. "They stayed behind to wait on the last of the luggage. Nice people, from what I can tell. Have you known them long?"

"This is the first time we'll meet," Rex confessed. "Count Vasile suggested we include them."

Sir Elmer tutted. "That man knows everyone who's anyone, that's for sure."

By then, the last guests emerged from the car. They had to be Mr and Mrs Murphy, a married couple in their early thirties, from what Dora knew of them. The man's suit had the cut of one off the rack, while the woman preferred Inga's favourite combination of blouse and cardigan. Their clothing was perfectly acceptable, but nothing to write home about. Dora shuddered to think about how Lady Lambert would react when she met everyone. Between herself, Ida Dixon, and middle-class Mrs Murphy, she'd end up with a very limited choice of companionship.

That thought brought a smile to Dora's face. She promised herself she'd be extra nice to these two women, to balance out the inevitable mistreatment from her hoity-toity ladyship.

It took one last round of introductions to put a name to every face. The weather was nice enough that they lingered on the doorstep while the footmen retrieved the luggage.

Dora chose that moment to offer her congratulations to Mr Murphy. "How does it feel to be one of the newly elected members of parliament?"

"Exhausting," he said, without missing a beat. "Don't get me wrong. I'm pleased as punch. However, your invitation for the weekend couldn't have come at a better time. Campaigning requires the energy of three men, despite being shouldered by one."

"Fortunately, we've left the afternoon free for everyone to rest from their journeys."

Mr Murphy's face lit up at this news, but Dora noticed his wife seemed less enthusiastic about the prospect. Mrs Murphy's gaze skimmed from one wing of the impressive manor to the other, revealing her longing to explore.

Dora didn't have anything pressing on her schedule. That left her free to take advantage of the opportunity to get to know one of their guests better. When Rex made for the door, inviting everyone inside, Dora hung back.

"Mrs Murphy, I was about to take a walk around the garden to stretch my legs while the weather holds. If you aren't in a rush to go upstairs, perhaps you'd like to join me."

Mrs Murphy was delighted by the offer. After a quick glance at her husband to make sure he had no reservations, she expressed her agreement.

Dora linked arms with Mrs Murphy and directed her onto the pathway leading to the gardens. "I insist you call me Theodora. May I call you, Gladys? I do so hate the formality of using surnames. I can't wait to show you the most delightful hidden bower I found yesterday in the water garden."

Gladys Murphy was putty in Dora's experienced hands. Although she was clearly overwhelmed by the grandeur of Ducklington, Dora's steady cadence and friendly tone put the woman at ease. By the time they reached the wooden bench Dora had in mind, they were on their way to becoming fast friends.

Chapter 4
The gruesome discovery

R ex was running late.
       In normal circumstances, Rex had no problem with
taking a more lackadaisical approach to schedules. But today, he
was on a mission, in the most literal sense of the word. Despite
his best efforts, he'd seen his planned arrival time for pre-dinner
drinks come and go. Here he was, still upstairs in his room,
standing like a statue while his valet faffed about with his tie
under the watchful eye of his cat Mews.

It took all of Rex's self-control not to shout at the poor man
or scowl at the cat. It wasn't Brantley's fault he was delayed. No,
the blame for that belonged on another doorstep.

As if to prove his point, just then the hidden door swung
open and his grandmother stepped inside. The cat took
advantage of the opportunity to escape into the secret
passageway. Rex half-wished he could follow.

The Dowager Duchess had on an evening dress of myrtle
velvet with lace detailing and long black gloves up to her
elbows. A double-strand of pearls hung from her neck, and
square-cut emerald and pearl earrings completed the look. She
eyed her grandson with a practiced eye before declaring, "He'll

do, Brantley. Would you mind checking whether Sir Elmer or Count Vasile need a hand with their final preparations?"

Brantley bobbed his head in recognition of the command and skedaddled out through the main door.

When the pair were alone, Rex forced his hands to relax. He checked his grandmother's face for any hint of why she was there. She was as impervious to his searching gaze as ever. There was nothing for it. He was going to have to come right out and ask. "Please tell me you have no more surprises up your sleeve, Grandmama. You know this is far more than a simple country-house party."

His grandmother bristled at his tone. "I'm fully cognisant of your rationale for being here. With the stakes as high as they are, I decided you needed all the help you could get."

"And that included you?"

The dowager scowled at the not-so-hidden subtext in his words. "Don't take that tone with me, young man. I bet Dora had a different reaction to the news of my arrival."

Rex grimaced. "I can't speak to her reaction, as I was unable to run her to ground. She and Inga disappeared on some mysterious undertaking. I searched for as long as I could, but eventually the chime of the clock sent me scurrying up here to dress."

The dowager stepped close and brushed a speck of dust from his ink-black jacket, just as she'd done since he was a small boy. "Leave Dora to me. If I don't catch her in her room, she's professional enough to deal with my arrival without falling to bits. I'll find a moment to explain before we go into dinner."

"It isn't your arrival that I'm concerned about. It's you choice of companion. Benedict Cavendish? Really, Grandmama! You know as well as I do that Dora and her brother are more prone to sniping at one another than getting along. While Dora might not bat an eyelash at you walking into the drawing room, she isn't going to have the same reaction when Benedict does!"

His grandmother didn't hesitate. "I had to bring someone, or else the numbers would be uneven! It wasn't as though I had much choice!" When Rex scoffed at her words, she squared her shoulders and faced him head on. "Reginald Arthur Bankes-Fernsby, have you forgotten who I am? I've been perfecting the art of intrigue since before your father was born. I will not tolerate you questioning my every decision."

Rex took a deep breath and let it out. Why was he so worked up about this? His grandmother held his gaze, silently asking the same thing.

He modulated his tone and tried to explain. "We've spent the last week planning every step of this. I'm not discounting the possibility of you being of assistance. What I am saying is it would have been nice to know you were coming before you arrived on the doorstep. So I could add you to our plans," he added, unnecessarily.

His grandmother shrugged off his concern. "Where's the fun in that?"

Rex wiped his hand over his face. "I never should have brought Dora home. I'm hard-pressed to say which one of you is a worse influence on the other."

"And that's the way we prefer it." The dowager glanced down and caught sight of his cufflinks. She tutted at his choice and rifled through his collection until she found a pair that was more to her liking. "Wear these."

She held the golden cufflinks engraved with the family crest in her palm, offering them in place of a peace offering. Rex hated to admit it, but they were a better choice than the simple pair he'd first selected. She'd made her point.

"Tell me how you'd like to help, Grandmama. I presume you've come with a specific role in mind."

"Lady Lambert." She laughed when Rex scowled at the mention of the woman's name. "My instincts were correct. Lillian Lambert is a snob of the worst kind. Although I have every confidence in Dora's capabilities, you are working on a limited timeline. With me here, giving my silent approval of Miss Laurent, Lillian will find it much harder to cause problems."

"But surely Dora being here, in your country home, is proof enough of your approval."

"For most of society, it would be sufficient. But Lady Lambert isn't the type to fall into line without a firm hand to shove her into place. As seemingly the highest rank woman in the house, she would be within her rights to decide how to treat the commoners. She's never been one to shy away for an opportunity to lord her status, particularly at the cost of someone else's happiness."

Rex contemplated her words. That certainly explained why Lady Lambert had gone to such efforts to snub Dora thus far. While Dora had expressed her annoyance, she hadn't flagged the lack of cordiality as a significant problem. That could only mean one thing...

"You told Dora to expect such behaviour, didn't you?"

His grandmother shrugged her shoulders. "I shared everything I knew about the guests. However, the more I thought about it, the greater I saw the risk of Lady Lambert getting her nose in a snit and deciding to leave early. That would have done more damage to your plans than my arrival."

She had him there. But there was still the matter of Benedict.

"Fine. I will grant you the win in that discussion. Now, will you tell me honestly why you added Benedict to the mix? Anyone else would buy your explanation of 'the numbers', but I know you too well to accept that as the truth. That game is nothing more than an excuse to add unmarried men to the dinner party. I hardly think we're in need of those here."

"There are many types of relationships, and marriage is only one of them. Brotherhood is the one on my mind. This rupture between Benedict and Dora is unhealthy. It is far past time for them to set aside their childish differences. Yet, all Benedict remembers is his heathen younger sister sticking out her tongue at all he holds dear. Dora is no better — she fights for freedom from a control Benedict isn't trying to exert. They need time together, forced proximity, to learn how to see past the children they were, and to the adults that they are."

"But now? This weekend, while Count Vasile is here?"

The dowager refused to back down. "Yes. Let Benedict glimpse his sister in action. If that doesn't change their view of one another, nothing will. Once the count and the other guests take their leave, we'll stay here for as long as it takes to get Benedict and Dora to see one another as allies instead of enemies."

Rex lifted his hand to run his fingers through his hair, but stopped himself before he could ruin the locks his valet had slicked into place. What was the point of arguing with an intractable, domineering... caring woman like his grandmother?

He'd talk to Dora and Inga, and get their thoughts on this turn of events. No point making a mountain of trouble if they viewed this as little more than a molehill.

He kissed his grandmother on the cheek, and she patted him on the arm. "We'd better go downstairs. Do you want to come with me?"

"No, I'll go back the way I came. It will be far more fun for me to appear dramatically in the drawing room on my own."

Rex was still chuckling when she closed the hidden door behind herself on the way out. He turned the other way, entering the main corridor at the same time as Sir Elmer opened the next door along. He stepped into the hallway and turned at the sound of Rex's hello.

"Ahh, Lord Rex. Thank you very much for sending your valet here to assist me. My tie wouldn't look half as good if I'd had to rely on my own skills."

"I share your shortcomings, Sir Elmer, so think nothing of it. Between you and me, I suspect Brantley creates these elaborate knots for the specific purpose of making himself invaluable."

"If that's the case, he's a success. Should you ever tire of his work, please point him in my direction."

Rex shook his head. "I wouldn't get my hopes up. Brantley has a position in my household for as long as he wants to stay. Speaking of, is he still in your room or did he move on to assist Count Vasile?"

"He was busy tidying the dressing area. I imagine he'll be along in a minute."

"In that case, I'll wait here to find out how much longer the count will be. Please, don't feel obliged to delay your arrival. I'm sure Miss Dixon will have her eye out for you."

Sir Elmer was happy enough to find his way downstairs. As soon as he was out of earshot, Rex gave a soft knock on Sir Elmer's door. Brantley opened it seconds later.

"Find anything of interest?"

"No, not unless you count the scuffs on his heels as relevant," the valet replied. "He should dismiss his valet for allowing him to leave the house in such a state."

Rex bit back a groan. This was the problem with bringing your valet into the spy's life rather than hiring a spy to act as valet. "Check whether the count has gone downstairs, will you?"

Brantley led the way to the count's assigned accommodations. He knocked on the door and listened, but received no reply. Rex waited outside of the line of sight and nodded for Brantley to go in.

The valet opened the door to reveal a dark room. "That's strange. Wouldn't he have left a lamp burning?"

"Surely he isn't still asleep." Rex pushed past Brantley and stuck his head through the doorway. "Count Vasile?"

There was no answer.

Rex edged into the darkened room. A faint metallic smell in the closed air caught his attention. It was far too familiar for Rex's liking.

He flicked on the lights and rushed across the room, hurrying toward the unmoving shape outlined by the bedcovers.

The count lay flat on his stomach, with his head turned to the side. His eyes were closed, looking to the world to be in a deep sleep.

Unfortunately for them all, the knife sticking from his back told a very different story.

Chapter 5
Too many surprises

The first two people Dora saw when she entered the drawing room were Ida Dixon and Lady Lambert. Their reactions to her entrance confirmed she'd made exactly the right choice of which evening gown to wear.

Ida gazed at Dora with profound admiration. Her mouth opened into a perfect O and the corners of her eyelids lifted in delight. Dora paused in the doorway, letting the light from the hall provide a stark, bright backdrop for the black dress.

Lady Lambert sucked in a breath, aghast at the overtly sensual gown that slithered over Dora's curves. She halted for a split-second, frozen in horror, before shifting her gaze to someone else in the room. Then, her expression morphed from disgust into the kind of savage, bloodthirsty smile that came when prey had no hope of escape.

That brought Dora up short. She stepped into the room, searching the space to see who or what made Lady Lambert feel so empowered. Lord Lambert... the Murphys... Inga...

And then she spotted someone unexpected.

In the wingback chair closest to the fire, looking completely at home in the drawing room's Victorian decor, sat none other than Lady Rockingham.

The dowager duchess herself.

Sirens rang in Dora's head as the pieces rearranged themselves on the game board. For the dowager to turn up with no warning only meant one thing. The woman was scheming. But to what end?

Dora got so caught up in solving that puzzle that she nearly missed the man standing behind the dowager. Benedict had come along as well? How did he fit into the picture?

The dowager made her move before Dora put her thoughts in order. She rose from her chair with a grace belying her age and made sure to catch Lady Lambert's eye.

Lady Lambert's mouth widened until it nearly dripped with venom. She fully expected the dowager to eviscerate Dora.

Dora held on to one certainty. The dowager stood in her corner. She didn't have anything to fear from her arrival, therefore, there was nothing for it except to proceed with a hello.

"Your Grace, what an unexpected pleasure finding you here."

"Please, Theodora, I asked you to call me Edith." The dowager exchanged air kisses with Dora and then took Dora's hands and stepped back so she could get a good look at Dora's dress. "This gown is a truly exquisite. The craftsmanship is second to none. You absolutely must tell me who designed it for you."

Lady Lambert actually spluttered when the dowager complimented Dora's dress. The dowager gave Dora's hands a quick squeeze to confirm that she knew exactly what she was doing. Dora could not stop the grin from spreading across her face.

That was why Rex's grandmother made the trek up from

London. She would take the odious responsibility for keeping Lady Lambert in check off Dora's shoulders.

The butler swooped in then and offered Dora a glass of champagne. Dora and the dowager clinked their glasses together in a silent toast, making it abundantly clear there'd be no fireworks coming from them.

With that question settled, everyone resumed their previous chatter. The dowager returned to her seat and started a conversation with Inga. Lady Lambert drowned her frustration in champagne and asked for a refill. Ida Dixon came over to pepper Dora with more questions about her dress. Dora answered them all and promised to introduce the young woman to the head of the Parisian house of couture.

When Sir Elmer arrived, Ida went to greet him, freeing Dora up to go speak with the Murphys. Dora slowly made her way around the room, checking with each of the guests to make sure that the rooms were to their liking. Eventually, she found herself standing in front of her brother.

"Lord Benedict, so nice of you to join us. I presume that Edith strong-armed you into accompanying her this weekend. I hope we haven't taken you away from anything too important."

"Not at all." His words sounded friendly, if one ignored the hard glint in his eye. "My parents are in the process of moving back into our London house. I'm relieved to have an excuse to get away from all the chaos."

Dora did not miss the subtext. Her parents were moving back in, and she was the one to blame.

Well, not entirely.

It was true that she and Rex had uncovered the mastermind behind a series of political machinations that left the House of Lords without a leader. As one of the senior-most Peers, Lord Cavendish had to step in. With his newly elevated status, he needed to be in London on a longer term basis.

Thus, the end was in sight for her brother's days of being a footloose bachelor. If having his parents under his roof wasn't enough to curtail his activities, his mother's attempts to find him a suitable bride would do the trick.

Dora almost pitied him, but couldn't bring herself to go that far. He'd lorded his status as eldest brother over her for most of her life, putting a stop to her childish adventures. It was about time someone did the same to him.

The footman saved Dora from having to make any further conversation with her brother. Archie, a member of her staff whom she had brought up for the weekend, gently cleared his throat to get her attention.

"I beg your pardon, madam, but you have a telephone call."

A telephone call? Dora tilted her head to the side, but Archie remained mum. Whatever was going on, he wouldn't say it in front of the others. Dora set her glass on the nearest side table, caught Inga's eye, and then left the room.

Her first thought was that it must be Lord Audley. Why he would phone her at this hour, especially given their current assignment, she couldn't say. She couldn't imagine him interrupting her evening for anything short of an emergency.

Her palms began to sweat as she followed Archie into the hallway. Instead of leading her to the telephone tucked in an alcove, he opened a hidden door and motioned for her to follow him upstairs.

"Lord Rex asked for someone to fetch you," he explained, once they were out of earshot of anyone else. "The matter is most urgent."

This did nothing to settle Dora's nerves. Her mind immediately went to work, running through the possibilities. Rex would not send Archie to find her for something as simple as a misplaced item or to tell her he was running late.

If she hadn't been so distracted by the appearance of the

dowager, she'd have noticed Rex's absence. And that of the count, now that she thought about it. Had Count Vasile confronted Rex because he'd somehow figured out what they were doing? Or, worse yet, had the man uncovered the network of spyholes and secret passageways in the house?

Dora mentally prepared herself for every eventuality while Archie led her to the count's bedroom. Every eventuality, that was, except to catch a whiff of the sharp scent of blood the moment she stepped inside. Her stomach cramped, and her eyes darted wildly around the room. She didn't breathe again until she saw Rex standing unharmed beside the fireplace.

His face was pale, but his hands were steady. "Dora, I'm so sorry." He stopped there and motioned toward the bed.

It was only then that Dora spotted the still form lying underneath the bedcovers. She locked onto the dagger and pool of blood staining the bedding. Even though she knew who it had to be, she was still somehow unprepared when she spotted the Count's far-too-pale face resting on the pillow.

"Oh no," she mumbled. "No, no, no..." Her voice trailed off the closer she got to the bed. She was no stranger to death, or even violent death, but this cut her to the bone. It wasn't just that Count Vasile was obviously dead. It was the position of his body, and the peaceful expression on his face.

She'd seen him lying in this exact position before, his face barely visible in the moonlight. That had been the moment she'd thought herself in love with him, and him with her. It was another week before she'd discovered he'd been playing her for a fool.

Despite that, she'd wanted to see Vasile beaten, not killed.

An uncontrollable shiver wracked her body. Rex rushed to her side and pulled her into his arms.

"Darling girl," he whispered.

Dora shushed him. She didn't need words of comfort right now, only a moment to pull herself together.

She clung to him. Thank heavens Rex wasn't the one lying dead. She listened to the steady cadence of his heartbeat, and in doing so, found a sense of stability.

He held still until her breathing slowed to something approaching normal. When she shifted position, he loosened his hold. "It's worst when it is someone we know. Brings back all the memories of the front."

His words cut through Dora's calm. He thought she'd been mourning Vasile.

She should have been thinking of the count. And yet, Rex had been the only one on her mind.

That realisation shocked her to her core. She pulled back from the comfort of his arms, stepping far enough away that she could no longer smell his cologne. This was no time for weakness, not with a man dead and a murderer under their roof. This was why she'd resisted her baser urges regarding Rex. Love fogged the mind in the moments when clarity was most needed.

She had to keep Rex at arms-length until she'd dealt with the situation.

Her resolve in place, she turned her mind back to business. "When did you discover him?"

"A few minutes ago," Rex replied. "I was running late... oh! My grandmama!"

"Yes, yes. She's here, and she brought Benedict along. I can't decide whether to curse or thank the almighty. We'll need her cool head to get through this, but having Benedict looking over our shoulders isn't going to help."

Rex gulped. "I hadn't even thought of that. As soon as I saw the count lying there, I sent Brantley to get you."

"He thought clearly enough to send Archie in with a pretext of an excuse, rather than bursting in with the news. It doesn't buy us much time, but we'd be fools to squander any advantage."

"Advantage? This is a disaster!"

He wasn't wrong, but Dora was hardly the type to let a wrinkle ruin her plans. "I will admit this is about as far from ideal as one can get, but if we keep our wits about us, we can find a silver lining."

Rex spluttered the start of an argument, but the firm set of Dora's mouth did the trick of shutting that down. He swallowed his ire and confessed, "I'm afraid the silver lining is eluding me at the moment."

"Then let me help you find it. First, we have a limited group of suspects. Two, we can keep them all here until we identify the murderer in our midst. Three, we have a strong inkling of the likely motive, which will help us solve the crime."

"Fine, but what about the police? We're not in London, with Lord Audley and his resources on a telephone call away. How are we going to get around that?"

Dora contemplated that question for a second. They definitely needed the police involved, or else they'd risk blowing their covers. But they couldn't phone just any police...

Lucky for them, they already had an officer on site.

"Harris will play the part of the local constable. He was away for most of the day, running errands in Oxford, so I highly doubt he crossed paths with any of our guests."

"Harris?" Rex heaved a sigh of relief. "Of course! I should have thought of him first."

"No, you did the right thing by sending for me," Dora said. She turned around to find Archie still waiting outside in the hallway. She motioned for him to come in and close the door.

Born and raised in the slums, Archie was no stranger to violence. He crossed his arms behind his back and stood at attention. "What can I do, Miss Laurent? Do you want me to fetch Harris and bring him here?"

"Eventually, but first, you and he will need to do some preparatory work. He'll need a uniform, a warrant card associated with the local constabulary, and a plain motor car. Get him, your sister, and your brother. Divide the work and give me a wave when everything is in place."

"What are we going to do?" Rex asked.

"We're going to tell everyone the bad news, and make careful note of their reactions. With any luck, well have a suspect in mind by the time Constable Harris arrives on the scene."

Chapter 6
Rex stands in the spotlight

Rex caught Dora's arm before she left the bedroom. "How do you want to handle the announcement? Do you want to tell them? The man was your friend. I barely met him."

"No, you need to be the one to say it, because you are the host. While all eyes are on you, I'll be free to study everyone's body language." She held out her hand. "To that point, pass me your handkerchief. A display of emotion ought to be enough to keep people from staring at me."

Dora stared off into the distance, blinking repeatedly until her eyes filled with tears.

What had crossed her mind? Rex wished she'd give word to her thoughts. He'd suspected Dora had been less than forthcoming about her previous encounters with Count Vasile. Watching the two of them interact that afternoon confirmed their past closeness. Dora knew how the count took his Scotch without needing to ask.

A lesser man would take offence at Dora keeping secrets. However, Rex had long since learned that Dora told people what was immediately relevant, and nothing else. There was no point pestering her for more information.

She'd looked for him as soon as she came into the room. Rex took great heart in that. More than anything she could have said, that action showed where her affection lay. Whatever had happened between Dora and the count was in the past. Rex was part of her present, and, with any luck, their connection would proceed into the future.

Yes, she'd pulled away at the end, but that was only because of the seriousness of their situation. He'd follow her lead.

"Should we search his things?" Rex asked, motioning to the stack of closed travel cases.

"Best wait and let Harris do it *officially*. Secure the door, though. Harris will have our hide if anything goes missing."

After locking the count's bedroom door, the pair took the main staircase to the front hall. Faint voices drifted from the nearby dining room, where the servants finished the preparations for dinner. Rex guided Dora in the other direction, to where their guests awaited them.

Dora emitted a perfectly timed sniffle as they entered the drawing room. All eyes turned their way and conversation ground to a halt. Dora distanced herself enough from Rex to move out of the line of sight, but still retain a good view of the room's occupants.

"Rex?" his grandmother asked. "What's happened?"

Rex composed his features. In a grim tone, he made the announcement. "I'm terribly sorry to be the bearer of bad news, but Count Vasile is no longer with us."

"He left?" asked Sir Elmer, confusion heavy in his voice.

Rex grimaced. He hadn't meant to mislead them. He cleared his throat and then blurted out the news. "Count Vasile is dead."

He was so focused on Sir Elmer that he forgot others were in the room until he heard the unmistakable crash of a glass hitting the floor. He and Sir Elmer turned their heads at the same time.

The butler's face was bright red as he rushed to apologise. "I jolted, and the glass wobbled right off the tray."

"It's understandable, Percival," Rex's grandmother hurried to reassure her trusted servant. "Rex caught us all off guard."

Sir Elmer wasn't about to be put off. He loosed a torrent of questions, talking right over the dowager. "When did you find out? How did it happen?"

The dowager raised a bejewelled hand and cut him off. "I'm sure Rex will answer all of your questions, Sir Elmer. But could we let him sit down first? In fact, I suggest we all do." She added, "Percival, please send someone to ask Cook to delay dinner."

Rex watched as the butler bowed at her command and departed to make the necessary rearrangements. He wished that he, too, could follow in his footsteps. But there was nothing to be done but carry on. Rex picked up a nearby wooden chair and carried it closer to the group. His grandmother, Inga, and Mr and Mrs Murphy were already sitting. Sir Elmer remained on his feet, standing behind Ida Dixon, with a hand resting on her shoulder. Lord Lambert guided his wife to the remaining settee.

Lord Benedict also stayed put. He kept still, positioned near the fire, part of the group but also somehow separate.

The remaining footman, one of Ducklington's servants, shifted a chair into place for Dora to use.

Rex took a moment to skim the room, grounding himself in the present. Starting from his left, Dora dabbed her eyes with his handkerchief, while Ida was nearly white as a sheet. Lord Lambert was suitably subdued. Lady Lambert had her lips pursed in displeasure, no doubt thinking how uncouth Rex was to allow a guest to perish under his roof.

Mrs Murphy fixed her gaze on her hands, where she twisted

her wedding band around in circles. Her husband appeared to be in shock. Rex's gut gave a lurch at the man's blank expression. He hurried on to look at Inga and his grandmother. Those two were as imperturbable as ever. That steadied his nerves.

"I will tell you what I saw, little that it is. I stopped by Count Vasile's room on my way downstairs. When I opened the door, the room was completely dark. I worried he'd overslept, but when I turned on the lights, I made a terrible discovery. I will spare you the details, but the death was not due to natural causes."

It took the occupants of the room a moment to understand the implications of what Rex had said. Mr Murphy reacted first.

"Egads, man! Are you saying he was murdered? Here? In this very house?"

Mrs Murphy laid a hand on her husband's leg. "I'm sure that isn't what Lord Rex meant."

Mr Murphy was having none of it. "How did he die? It couldn't have been a gunshot, as we'd have all heard that."

"Poison?" Inga said, before her better sense kicked in. She hunkered lower in her seat and sealed her lips. The damage, however, was done. Almost as one, the guests eyed their half-empty drink glasses. Rex tossed Dora a frantic glance, hoping she'd intervene to get the discussion back on track.

"There was blood," she wailed. That was an easy enough cue to interpret.

Rex cleared his throat to quiet everyone down. "Someone stabbed Count Vasile. We've phoned the county constabulary and they're sending an officer. Until then, I must ask you to all stay put."

"Stay put?" Lady Lambert shrieked. "I think not! I won't relax for a second knowing there is a murderer hiding among the servants."

"I beg your pardon?" the dowager replied in a frosty tone. "My servants have more to fear from you than vice versa. Most of them didn't even meet the man."

Lady Lambert didn't back down. "Perhaps one of them is deranged? How am I to be cognisant of the problems with your help? If you insist on the murderer being a guest, I'd look at Miss Laurent and Miss Dixon. Breeding will out, I always say."

Ida Dixon recoiled under the insult and burst into heaving sobs. Sir Elmer pulled her into his arms while he glared daggers at Lady Lambert. "My Ida is no killer. She hadn't met the count, either."

"Then it must be Miss Laurent," Lady Lambert insisted. "I find it very suspicious that Miss Laurent was the last to arrive for drinks, and then Lord Rex discovers the body. You have only to look upon her to recognise she is a devil in disguise."

"Lillian Lambert!" The dowager's voice sliced through the room. "I strongly suggest you cease speaking now before you say something else you will regret. The only person behaving badly here is you."

"Well, I never!" Lady Lambert leapt to her feet and spun to face Rex's grandmother. "Has old age finally taken its toll on your mental facilities? First you allow that woman into your home, and now you defend her? I won't stand here and listen to this. Come along, Laurence. We'll lock ourselves in our room until it is safe to emerge."

Lord and Lady Lambert brushed past Rex without a word of goodbye. He debated whether he should stop them, but quickly put that idea to bed. At the rate Lady Lambert was going, his grandmama was likely to off her.

Their departure dispelled some of the tense atmosphere in the room. Mrs Murphy offered to escort the still-crying Ida Dixon to the powder room. Sir Elmer watched helplessly as his companion left the room. Although Lady Lambert caused Ida's sorrows, Sir Elmer turned a heated glare Rex's way.

"That woman is a ninny, but she has raised a fair point. This is your home, and you found the body. Yet, you'd have us believe you weren't involved."

Rex rocked backward, sure he'd misheard. "Are you suggesting I killed Count Vasile? What possible motive would I have?"

"Her!" Sir Elmer replied. He lifted his hand and pointed directly at Dora. "Vasile told me enough that I was able to read between the lines. He and Miss Laurent had some sort of history." Sir Elmer sat up straighter, warming to the idea. "I bet you didn't know that! What happened, Lord Rex? Did you stumble across them in a compromising position? Was that when you realised Miss Laurent had been less than forthcoming about her past?"

Rex opened his mouth to retort, but where to start first?

He needn't have worried. Once again, the dowager duchess took control, rushing to her grandson's defence.

"Utterly preposterous! If Theodora wanted to be with the count, she is under no obligation to stay here. She'd have to be a complete fool to carry on with two paramours under the same roof. The same stands for Rex. My grandson is not blind to Theodora's past. Even if he'd planned to murder his rival, why would he do so here and now?"

Sir Elmer's cheeks burned, but he didn't slump or retract his accusation. "Preposterous or not, your grace, you can rest assured that I will raise this possibility with the constable once he arrives. And on that note, I will excuse myself to check on Ida."

Was this what it was like to guide a ship through a typhoon? In the span of a few minutes, Rex had suffered emotional battery, had his reputation skewered, and his presumed love interest insulted twice-over. The urge to throw his hands in the air and storm out was overwhelming.

Patrick Murphy's words brought Rex back to the present. Rex had all but forgotten the man was still there.

"You must forgive Sir Elmer. He and Count Vasile have been close friends ever since the war. In his shoes, I'm not sure I'd react any better."

Drat. The man was right. In the heat of the moment, Rex had forgotten about the two men's shared history. Rex covered his face with his hands to buy himself a moment to clear his thoughts. He and Dora hadn't discussed what to do beyond sharing the news.

The dowager duchess intervened. "Rex, can I leave you to wait for the constable? I'd like to retire to my room. Benedict, would you be so kind as to lend me your arm while I climb the stairs?"

Like Rex, Benedict no doubt knew the dowager was fully capable of managing the stairs on her own. Nonetheless, he gave in with no argument, circling around her chair to offer her his arm.

The dowager wasn't done issuing commands. "Percival," she said, to get the butler's attention. "If it isn't too much trouble, would you arrange for dinner to be served on trays in everyone's room? It's best we let tempers cool before we ask our guests to break bread together."

"Of course, your grace. I'll see to it at once."

Mr Murphy followed behind Benedict and Lady Rockingham. In short order, Rex found himself in the company of only Dora and Inga. Even the footman had left the room.

Inga got up and went to the drinks cart. She poured a healthy serving of whiskey into two glasses and then delivered them to Rex and Dora.

"Drink up," she said, standing watch until they did as told.

"We'll have a long night in front of us once Harris arrives to play his part in this unscripted farce of a weekend."

Rex's head snapped up from where he'd been staring into his glass. "How'd you guess we called Harris?"

Inga shook her head at his naivety. "You've got a dead spy and a house full of suspects. There was no question in mind which officer you'd ring. That doesn't solve our bigger problem."

Bigger than a murder? Rex felt his stomach clench. "What's that?"

Inga answered his question, but she did so while looking at Dora. "What in the world are we going to do about Benedict?"

Chapter 7
Inga to the rescue

rchie put in a brief appearance to tell them how long they had before Harris's big arrival scene. Thus reassured they had time to spare, Dora, Inga, and Rex withdrew from the drawing room and headed upstairs to change into more comfortable clothing.

Despite Inga's last question, Dora wasn't worried about her brother. She closed her bedroom door and slipped off her heels. She wanted nothing more now than to get out of her dress.

When she'd put it on, she'd felt like a goddess. She'd descended the main staircase with one plan in mind. She couldn't wait to see the look on Vasile's face when she walked through the drawing-room door.

Now, the dress made a mockery of her. Funeral black had never been more appropriate.

Nothing had gone as she'd expected. Her need for control demanded she identify when everything went wrong.

While she replayed the events of the day, Dora lifted her hands to undo the buttons running along the back of the gown. She fumbled her way through the first few, remembering her first conversation with the count. Had he seemed worried or on edge?

All she recalled was how tired he'd been. She dug deeper into her memories, refining the image of him relaxing on the settee. She skipped her gaze between him and Rex. Rather than arriving at a flash of insight, she hit upon a stumbling block - mental and physical.

She remembered everything about Rex — how he was sitting, the way he'd laughed at a joke.

But the finer details of Count Vasile refused to come into focus. It was just as out of reach as the fourth button of her dress.

She began again, starting from the bottom. Her nimble fingers flew up the back of her dress until she hit yet another hitch. No matter which way she contorted herself, she couldn't reach the fourth and fifth buttons. As she wriggled and moved, her breathing grew ragged. The fabric pulled tight against her chest.

The dress refused to let her go. It clutched her in its tight embrace, holding her to account for her role in this tragedy. The moment her gaze landed on the empty glass on her side table, the truth punched her in the gut.

She'd been so clever to add the relaxation potion to the count's drink. She'd wanted him out of the way, so she and Rex could work freely. Her actions ensured Vasile slept like the dead. If it wasn't for her, would he still be alive?

Dora glimpsed her frantic motions in the mirror and nearly fell to pieces.

It was a knock on her bedroom door that saved her from herself.

Inga didn't wait for an answer before entering. She took one look at Dora and hurried to her side. "Let me help you get out of that dress."

Inga's no-nonsense tone gave Dora the strength to stand straight. She stood perfectly still while Inga's fingers undid the last two buttons.

"Do you want me to stay with you?" Inga asked, while still standing at Dora's back.

Dora lifted her gaze and focused on her bedroom door, but it was another room holding court in her mind's eye. Part of her longed to have Rex here, instead of her dear friend Inga.

It was worse than she feared. Dora no longer trusted herself to be alone with Rex. Especially not now, while the investigation was kicking off.

Count Vasile would haunt her forever if she didn't confess her sin. She had to tell someone what she'd done. Inga would understand. In a small voice, she admitted, "It's my fault."

"What's your fault?" Inga asked.

"Vasile's death."

"Because... you stabbed him?" Inga nudged Dora's shoulder to turn her around. Inga looked her in the eye and gave a firm shake of her head. "That can't be true because you weren't even in the house for most of the afternoon. Mrs Murphy regaled me with the list of the places you showed her on the property. Then I dragged you away to help me gather cuttings for my potions. Unless you snuck in and stabbed him while getting dressed, I can't see how you accomplished this crime."

That wasn't what Dora had meant, and Inga knew it. Dora shook free of Inga's grasp and moved behind the screen to get changed. Out of sight, she made her confession. "I dosed Vasile with your relaxation powder before sending him upstairs to rest. If I hadn't drugged him, he would have woken up when the killer came into this room. He could have called out, or fought back..."

"Or nothing. He's dead. You aren't to blame," Inga said, cutting into Dora's monologue. "That powder isn't strong enough on its own to knock anyone out. You told me yourself that he said he was exhausted."

"Perhaps..." The word tasted like ash in Dora's mouth. She'd never been one to blame herself for actions outside her control, but this warranted an exception. He wasn't that hard a sleeper. If it weren't for her split-second decision to doctor his drink, he'd have woken up. She was responsible for taking away his fighting chance.

Dora slipped out of the black gown and hung it over the top of the screen. It would be a long time before she would wear it again. Where it had once looked ethereal and awe-inspiring, now all she could see was the deep black permanency of death.

"You should go eat," Dora said to Inga. Her voice gave away none of the regret she suffered. "Harris will be here soon enough."

"I asked the housemaid to deliver my food here. We'll eat together." Inga stuck her head around the side of the screen and didn't bat an eyelash at the sight of Dora in her underclothes. "In the meantime, you will cease beating yourself up for things that happened in the past."

Dora grabbed her Chinese silk robe and wrapped it around herself. "Oh, is that all? Shall I arrange for world peace and eliminate hunger while I'm at it? As well you know, life is full of regrets. I wouldn't be human if I didn't self-flagellate every now and again."

"Oh, please!" Inga groaned. "The only flagellation you enjoy is the kind involving someone else."

Dora's cheeks flushed as an image of a handsome man in a darkened bedroom came to mind. How dare Inga distract her with such an inappropriate thought! Dora gave her the evil eye as she swanned past.

Inga replied by swatting Dora's backside. Dora spun around and lifted her hand in a silent threat. The women locked eyes and burst out laughing. It was impossible to remain melancholic when the two of them were together.

Dora gave Inga a quick squeeze to show her thanks before walking to her dressing table. She took off one earring and then the other, taking care to put them away in her jewellery case.

Inga moved around to lean against the wall beside the dressing-table mirror, standing where she could look Dora in the eye. "Now that you're back to your normal temperament, I will admit that I don't like this."

"No one likes murder, Inga."

"That isn't what I meant, and you know it. Murder is something with which we have a fair amount of experience. What worries me is that there are far too many complications here."

"Starting with Benedict," Dora said. "Drat Edith for bringing him along. Why do you think she did so?"

"The answer is obvious."

Dora contemplated the question for a moment. She arrived quickly enough at an answer, but it didn't entirely make sense. "The dowager wants us to be friends?"

"I suspect this is more about your mother's wishes, than those of Rex's grandmother. I watched your mother carefully during the night of your first dinner together. There were so many times when she looked at you, and then at Benedict, and back at you again. Her desire to have her family fully reunited was writ large across her face for anyone to see."

Dora didn't like the way Inga's response made her feel. Mostly because she knew she was right. Her mother had long entertained dreams of her three children playing together nicely. She'd turned a blind eye to Benedict's habit of bossing his younger siblings around. She'd also ignored Dora's and Will's efforts to wind Benedict up. With Dora back in England, her mother was grasping at any straw that might bring her a step closer to finally realising that dream.

As to what Dora and Benedict thought of this plan, that was irrelevant.

Dora had far too much on her plate to deal with this problem now. The best solution for everyone involved would be for Benedict to make himself scarce. She turned to Inga. "We'll have Harris send him away."

"You say that as though you are expecting it to work. He is your brother, Dora. Even if none of the other guests are aware of the connection between you two, I still doubt he will exit stage right simply because you ask nicely... or order him, for that matter."

Dora brushed the implied criticism aside. "What would you have me do? Tell him the truth? There's no point to that. He's hell-bent on seeing me as an aimless young woman jumping from one adventure to another. I'm far too old to waste time defending myself when his opinion ultimately doesn't matter."

"Be that as it may, your determination to keep the more admirable side of your work a secret from him is now biting you in the rear." Inga crossed her arms. "Let me simplify this choice for you. Either you ask Archie and Basel to physically bind Benedict's arms and legs and bodily carry him out the back door... or you stop acting like a child and tell him the truth."

Dora scowled at Inga again. "No grey area? No middle ground?" When Inga's lips stayed sealed, Dora huffed in frustration. "And you say I'm stubborn. As much as the mental picture of the former option entertains me, I'm guessing you want me to do the latter."

Inga uncrossed her arms and reached out a hand to bop Dora on her pert nose. "And they said you weren't that intelligent!"

"Ha ha. Tell me, oh great master, how much do I have to share with Benedict?"

"As much as is needed. The few times in the past when you've shared only part of the information, how well has that worked for the other person? You're going to have to come clean with Benedict. Doing anything less puts him at risk. Sleeping under the same roof as a murderer trumps any need for secrecy."

"Have I mentioned lately how much I detest it when you counter my nonsense with logical arguments?" Dora closed her jewellery case and tucked it away in the drawer. "I will follow your suggestion, but I'd like it noted for the record that I vehemently disagreed."

"Of course you did," Inga murmured while patting Dora on the head.

Dora flashed back to her childhood when her mother instructed her to play nice with her older brother. Then, just as now, she'd promised to change her ways. Deep inside, however, she remembered that fruitful conversations required openness on both sides. If there was one thing Benedict didn't have, it was an open mind when it came to her.

Benedict's disapproval of her stood like a mountain between them. A gentle approach wasn't going to do the trick. As she ate her meal, Dora girded her loins. The next time she saw him, she would sling her words with the force of a sledgehammer.

Chapter 8
Benedict stands his ground

M eanwhile, in another part of the house...
Rex walked into his bedroom and closed the door.
After the emotional outburst and angry taunts tossed about in
the drawing room, Rex welcomed the silence of his private
space.

It didn't take long for the silence to grate on his nerves. With
no one and nothing to distract him, Rex forced himself to
contend with the enormity of their situation. It wasn't just that
the count was dead. Somehow, Rex sat atop the suspect list.

Obviously, he was not the murderer, but he recognised that
Harris might have to treat him as though he were. Doing
anything else would arouse suspicion amongst the guests.

There was nothing he could do about that now. Instead, he
turned his attention to the task of getting changed. Rex
wandered into his dressing room and shuffled through the
clothing until he found a pair of trousers and a simple shirt. By
the time he finished dressing, a footman was there with a dinner
tray. Knowing he had limited time, Rex ate it as fast as he could,
hardly tasting the expertly prepared meal.

He was staring into the fire, watching the last of his wine

swirl around within his glass, when he heard a light knock on his door.

"Come in," he said, assuming it was the footman back for the tray.

It wasn't a servant. Benedict Cavendish stepped over the threshold.

Like Rex, Benedict was tall, with blond hair and an athletic build. He was a chip off the old block, with the family's green eyes, and a strong, square jawline marked by a cleft chin. Many a young woman's heart went pitter patter at the thought of them. However, women were the furthest thing from their minds.

Benedict took a few steps into the room after making sure the door was fully closed. He stared at Rex as though examining a stranger.

Rex shifted uncomfortably, not liking the sharp edge to Benedict's gaze. When he could stand it no longer, he spoke. "Can I help you with something, Lord Benedict?"

"What game are you playing here?" Benedict said, practically bristling.

Rex viewed him askance. "None of which I am aware."

"So she has conned you as well," Benedict muttered, half to himself. "It's good that I came to speak with you."

Rex froze, not liking the direction of the conversation. "Who has conned me?"

"My sister," Benedict spat. "You needn't be embarrassed about it. She's highly skilled. The average man stands little chance against her when she engages her feminine wiles."

Rex held up a hand. "Where are you getting your information? I assure you, I am not a victim of anyone, least of all your sister. You do her and me both a disservice by assuming her seduction skills are the only reason I'd be with her."

Benedict's lips flattened. He tilted his head to the side and studied Rex anew. "You're serious. Why? She's a daredevil, driven by nothing other than the thrill that comes from taking risks. She flaunts herself around the world, thumbing her nose at us. The truth is, she cares for no one but herself! She'll ruin you, man!"

Rex pitied Benedict. His blind rage at his sister prevented him from seeing the woman she'd become. Underneath the frustration and anger lay a deeper emotion. Somewhere inside, Benedict cared about Dora. That compelled Rex to continue the conversation rather than showing Benedict the door.

"You drastically underestimate Dora. Yes, every move she makes is calculated to the nth degree, but that isn't for her own benefit. Hidden beneath her sequinned and bejewelled surface lies a woman absolutely dedicated to her cause."

Benedict contemplated Rex's words for a moment. His eyes flicked from side to side as he thought through the implications. "You say she planned this, and you went along willingly?"

Rex gave a single nod.

"Then who killed Count Vasile? Was it you or her?"

"What?" Rex spluttered.

"Game or not, it is clear to me that you arranged this weekend in order to lure the man to his death. The only question is which one of you raised a hand for the final blow?"

"I did."

Rex spun around at Dora's words. He hadn't heard her come in, but there she stood beside the open door to the hidden passageway. She strode in with nary a care for how her shocking words landed.

Inga followed close behind. Unlike Dora, she was unable to hide her sentiments. Her mouth was pinched and her nose flared as she huffed. But whether she was angry with Dora or Benedict, Rex couldn't say.

Dora kept walking, getting ever closer to her brother. She

was deep in character, with her head tilted high and a devil-may-care air.

Benedict was apoplectic with rage. His face practically glowed red. He'd balled his hands into fists and kept them tucked against his side.

Rex took half a step to intervene, but Inga laid a hand on his arm to stay him. She shook her head when he glanced over. While Rex had no idea what game Dora was playing with Benedict, Inga seemed to have some clue. The tightness in his shoulders eased.

Despite Benedict's aggressive stance, Dora showed no signs of fear. She sauntered around Benedict, practically daring him to come after her. "You wanted a confession, so there you have it. Consider it a gift. I'm guilty. Now you can see the horrific spectre of Theodora Laurent locked away for eternity. I'm sure you think the only question remaining is whether you can coerce me into going quietly. But I have one for you. Tell me, Benedict, does my answer make you happy?"

Benedict shuddered as her words landed like blows. "You think I want you gone that badly? This is my worst nightmare come true! Lady Rockingham attempted to convince me of your innocence, but I knew better than to allow false hope to take hold. You mock me with your words, but it is no matter. Lord Rex had already confirmed my worst fears before you arrived."

Rex couldn't remain silent in the face of such an accusation. "I did no such thing!"

"Didn't you, though? You said Dora plans and calculates, all to support some higher cause. Here we are, in the countryside, with a group of people who are practically strangers. I'd be a fool not to see that she dragged you here on one of her alleged missions. Yet, you'd have me believe that the murder was an accident? Somehow, someone else came into your controlled environment and wiped out one of the players? Either Dora is a mastermind, or she is not. Which is it?"

Rex growled. Why was Benedict being so obtuse? He wanted to shake the man.

Dora, however, was unfazed. She looked at Rex. "Don't let Benedict goad you with his circular logic."

"Goad him?" Benedict shook his head. "I cannot believe anyone would sanction a cold-blooded murder. I ask for honesty so I can save you both from the hangman's noose."

"Why?" Dora asked, keeping her tone carefully moderated.

Benedict was happy to explain. "Because our family has suffered enough. I won't watch Mama mourn another child. Tell me the truth of your involvement and tell me fast. I'll use every tool at my disposal to help you get away."

"Away?" Dora strode over to Benedict and poked her finger at him. "Of course, it always comes back to banishment with you. Don't pretend this is for Mama. You want the truth so you can see me gone for your own selfish reasons... your title, your reputation, and your future generations. You have never cared to look past your own nose. It was far easier to turn a blind eye to my desires than to go to the trouble of accommodating them. This is why we go round and round every time we're together. It is also why I keep you in the dark."

"You lie to me!" Benedict blurted. "Don't pretty it up."

Dora's expression softened. "I've kept you safe from the truth because it is a heavy burden. However, a wise friend tells me that the time for honesty has come. If you want the truth about my role in Vasile's death, I will tell you. But you must make that choice. I won't make it for you."

Benedict's shoulders loosened. He gazed off into the distance, pondering Dora's question, while absentmindedly rubbing his hands on his trousers.

Inga leaned close to Rex and whispered, "It's about time she got around to her point." Her words did little to assuage Rex's concerns.

Benedict rubbed his temples before finally giving in to his curiosity. "I'm sure I'll end up regretting this, but fine, I'll listen to your tale."

"Our time is short, so forgive me for opting for brevity. Although you won't find my name, assumed or real, on any official list, I work on behalf of our government. For the last five years, I've gone into rooms and taken part in conversations that are off-limits to diplomats. My duties have included delivering messages, gathering intelligence, stealing information, and eliminating foreign spies."

Benedict crossed his arms. "Try again."

"I'm sorry?" Dora's forehead creased with her frown.

"Try again, only this time don't tell me another one of your imaginary tales. I know all about the government's new spy agency, and you are most definitely not part of it."

Dora reared back. "I never said I was. Were you not paying attention? I told you I wasn't on any list. That is as much for your protection as for mine."

Benedict remained unconvinced. "Dora, you've been playing these kinds of games since we were children. There are no 'off the books' spies. Our father is the leader of the House of Lords. I'm no political newcomer. If such a thing as you suggest existed, I would have been told."

Rex sensed that if he didn't intervene, they'd continue in this vein all night. "Benedict, if you won't believe her, then give me a chance. We invited Count Vasile here for the express purpose of uncovering his employer. Murder was not in the cards. Someone else has shuffled the deck. Now, we must not only uncover who killed Vasile, but also what the murderer needs to hide. You can stay and render your assistance, or you can get out before this situation further deteriorates."

Rex took care to avoid catching Dora's eye. He didn't need to see her face to know she was livid with the way her brother was treating them. She'd put Benedict in his place soon enough. For now, they had bigger fish to fry.

For his part, Benedict took his time considering the question. He walked over to the window and pulled back the curtains. At this late hour, the view was limited. Yet something caught Benedict's eye.

"There is a car coming up the drive. The police?"

No one disagreed.

Benedict stepped back and let the curtain fall shut. He turned around and faced his sister. "I'll stay for long enough to see what you are up against before I make my final decision. Unless you intend to bring the officer here, I suggest we move to a more appropriate setting."

"The library," Rex said, automatically. When Benedict glanced his way, Rex added, "It is the most private room in the house."

They barely had time to make it downstairs before the doorbell rang with a peal that echoed through the front hall. The butler stood at attention, awaiting instruction.

"Percival, give us a moment to get settled in the library and then show him in," Rex instructed.

The butler inclined his head, keeping otherwise silent while the group filed past.

The library was a cosy, inviting space, with bookshelves lining the walls and comfortable armchairs for seating. The decor featured leather and velvet in rich, autumnal colours. A large desk occupied one corner, but Rex directed the group toward the seating area beside the fireplace.

Despite the decor, the change of venue did little to relieve the tension. Rex took his place beside Dora on the sofa, leaving the other chairs for Benedict and Inga. Harris's timely arrival would surely shift everyone's focus back to the mission.

Percival followed his instructions to a tee. He knocked on the door and announced their new arrival. "Constable Harris from the Gloucestershire Constabulary is here to see you, my lord." With that done, he made his exit.

Rex kept his expression neutral while Harris came into the room. Harris had on a hat and coat typical of a police detective's budget, made of fine-quality materials but not tailored to his measurements. Harris swept the hat from his head and bowed to Dora and Inga.

Dora and Inga took one look at the firelight reflecting off Harris's bald head and tittered their amusement. For his part, Rex struggled to keep a straight face. It was exactly the moment of levity they all needed.

Benedict had to ruin it.

His eyes widened, and he spluttered in shock. "Dora, why is your butler masquerading as a police officer?"

Chapter 9
Playing the role of Constable

Despite Benedict's obvious consternation, Dora was unperturbed. She waved for Benedict to lower his voice. "If you'd listened to me before, you'd have the answer. I am a spy, and my so-called household is actually my team. No one is exactly as they appear. Harris has plenty of experience being a police officer, so he should have no problem doing a convincing job of the role. Isn't that correct, Harris?"

Benedict's scowl reemerged. He was gearing up for another one of his endless rounds of argument.

Harris, however, put paid to that plan. He helped himself to the chair beside the desk and moved closer to the group. "I've been around you long enough to come prepared for every eventuality, no matter how farfetched. I had my old suit in my case. Still fits me like a glove."

"I believe the credit for that belongs to me, dear. If I allowed you to indulge in as many custard creams as you wanted, you'd have no hope of buttoning those trousers."

"Never mind that," said Harris, cutting off Inga before she could do further damage to his reputation. "I hopped into action as soon as the boys tracked me down. I take it from the chaos below stairs that you opted to cancel dinner and instead alerted the guests to Count Vasile's demise."

"We didn't have a plausible explanation for why the count was absent," Dora explained. "The news went down about as well as you can imagine. Sir Elmer, among others, was quick to share his suspicions. He pointed the finger at Lord Rex, offering jealousy as a motive."

Harris grimaced. "The green-eyed monster has been responsible for many a crime, but at least that isn't the case here. I'll have to be quick to put those to bed. I need you two free to gather information. No one will speak to you if they suspect Rex is guilty."

Benedict coughed. "Sorry to be the one to interject reality into this situation, but are you out of your bloody minds?" He glanced around at the others, waiting for one of them to agree. When they all stared back at him, unmoved by his pronouncement, he leapt to his feet. "We have a dead man lying in a guest bedroom, a butler playing pretend, and now a ridiculous plan to investigate on your own. You're going to end up in prison, the whole lot of you, or the madhouse. Frankly, I'm not sure which one is more appropriate!"

"Benedict Francis Cavendish! How dare you!" Dora gasped.

"Pipe down, both of you," Harris growled. He pointed a finger at Dora. "From the way you spoke earlier, I assumed you'd told Benedict everything."

"We did," Dora fumed. "I told him. Rex confirmed. You've backed me up. But he is steadfast in his refusal to see reason."

"Reason is why I'm acting now to put a stop to this," Benedict said. He lifted his hands and appealed to the group. "You can still call the local constabulary. No one has to learn Harris feigned being a part of their force. No harm, no foul. We turn the investigation over to the professionals."

Dora was so livid that she was sure her eyes were going to cross. Why did Benedict have to be so obtuse? This was exactly why she and Will had gone to such elaborate efforts to avoid spending time with their older brother. All he cared about were rules and reputations.

Perhaps, however, that was a lever she could use against him.

"Have you thought through what would happen if we played it your way?" Dora levelled her gaze at her brother. "The son of the Earl of Rockingham accused of murder. His girlfriend unmasked as none other than the missing Cavendish girl. The papers will run out of ink before this story falls out of fashion. We'll be ruined. All of us." Especially you...

She waited a beat, and then another. However, Benedict had run out of words. "I explained why we can't call in a real investigation team. There's more at stake here than identifying a murderer. I promise, there's no one in England better qualified to take on this assignment. You must stop seeing me as your baby sister and view me as a trained professional."

Rex added his support. "You are of no use to us if all you plan to do is underestimate our abilities. Our crew has undertaken three murder investigations together. Goodness knows what Dora has done in the years before her return to England. She is not pulling your leg when she says she is more experienced than you can imagine."

"Fine," Benedict spat. "There is no talking you out of this. However, I can hardly leave you here on your own. Someone has to rein you in. Since we have investigators galore and the police on hand, what happens next?"

Harris took that as his cue. He got up from his chair and motioned for the others to follow. "It's time for me to view the crime scene. Ladies, please keep your tears and emotional outbursts in the corridor. Rex, you can show me to the scene."

"What about me?" Benedict asked.

Harris glared at him, using the steely gaze he had perfected in his previous life as a detective. "For now, you must stay out of the way. Let me do my part and set the stage for what will happen over the rest of the weekend."

Benedict snapped his mouth shut and gave a terse nod of understanding. "In that case, I'll remain here to read."

"Start with the third shelf from the bottom, closest to the desk," Dora said. "That's where you'll find the detective novels."

Dora watched with satisfaction as her brother covered his face with his hands and groaned. Despite his words, Dora remained unconvinced about whether he would truly lend a hand.

With Benedict, actions had always spoken louder than words. Many a time, he had played the role of a friend in order to gain information he later turned against them. Inga said to trust him, but Dora wasn't ready to go that far. Not until he proved he'd keep an open mind when it came to her.

Harris paused before leaving the room. With his back to the door, he tapped his chin. "How to play this... bumbling countryside copper is out of the question. Straight-shooter?"

Inga elbowed him to get his attention. "As much as it pains me to admit this, the time has come for you to take on the role you always wanted to play."

Harris's eyes lit up. "Loud-mouth, brash detective with a take-no-prisoners attitude? But you hate it when I act that way."

"And that's why it's perfect now. Go ahead. You have my blessing."

Inga didn't need to say that twice. Harris spun around and swung the door open with more force than was strictly required. His booming footsteps echoed as he marched off. Dora, Rex, and Inga had to rush to keep up.

When they reached the upper floor where the guest

bedrooms were located, he growled. "Well, where is the corpse? Stabbed in the back, you say? That's a little too spot on for your crowd, eh, your lordship?"

Dora turned on the waterworks, and Inga pulled her into an embrace.

"Get her out of here," Harris demanded. "That's what you get for letting her see the body. You'll be paying for that for weeks!"

"Err, yes, sir. I mean, right this way." Rex bumbled along, pretending to be out of his depth. "The count's room is up ahead."

Dora continued to sniffle while walking along the carpeted hallway. She noted the shadows moving under the doors of their other guests. Excellent! Their audience was paying attention. She tapped Inga's arm and nodded toward Rex's doorway. It was the perfect spot for them to keep watch.

Rex and Harris finally arrived at the count's room. Dora and Inga slid behind them and walked a few steps further to where they could huddle near Rex's door. From there, Dora had a front-row seat to Harris's show.

Harris grabbed the doorknob and attempted to twist it. "It's locked!"

"I thought that best, Detective," Rex explained. "I was sure you wouldn't want anyone messing with the scene of the crime."

"Other than you," Harris said, pointing his finger against Rex's chest. "You, your valet, your lady friend over there. As my grandfather used to say, there's not much point in locking the barn door once the horses are out."

"It wasn't like that," Rex protested in ringing tones. "My valet went in to offer assistance, but all the lights were off..."

"Yes, yes, you already explained. Be a good man and hand me the key. I'll see for myself, if you don't mind."

Rex pulled a large, round keyring from his pocket and

flipped through the keys until he found the one he wanted. He handed it to Harris.

"Is this some kind of tree on the key?"

"It's a Hawthorn. For the Hawthorn room." Rex pointed at the others. "Each key is marked with the symbol of the relevant room."

"Hmm, not much of a security feature," Harris said. "I suppose you need some method for keeping track when you've got this many rooms under your roof. But have you considered how easy it is for someone to determine which key unlocks each door?"

"I hadn't thought of that," Rex said. He glanced at Dora and she gave a quick shake of her head. "It's irrelevant in this case. The door was unlocked when we found him."

"More useful to know whether the count locked it before laying down to rest. No way of determining that now, however. Alright, stand back. I'll go in on my own." Harris put the key in the lock, opened the door, and then shut it in Rex's face.

The silence of the hallway rang as loud as the previous voices. Dora heard the scrape of a lock turning. She glanced across the way in time to see Sir Elmer emerge from his room.

Sir Elmer eyed the women first, and then Rex. Like them, he had changed out of his formal evening wear. His thick jumper emphasised his muscled arms, but his bloodshot eyes betrayed his grief.

"That the police?" he asked. Rex nodded. "Took them long enough to send someone. I was thinking you hadn't actually called."

Rex wrinkled his brow. "Despite your suspicions, I am not responsible for the count's death. I want to see the culprit identified as much as you do, perhaps more."

"We'll see," was all Sir Elmer replied.

Dora couldn't abide Sir Elmer's recalcitrance. She was

willing to give him a certain amount of leeway since the count was a dear friend. But the longer he stood around, tossing accusations at Rex, the harder it would be to get him to have an open mind.

Inga still had an arm around her shoulders. Dora pulled free and moved away from her friend.

"Sir Elmer," she said, to get the man's attention. "I've had about enough of you pointing the finger at Rex. The only thing he's guilty of is indulging my every request. I was all set to return to London so I could catch up with my old friend when Rex offered to play host. He was under no duress to open his home to you and the others. He did so out of the goodness of his heart, and this is how you repay him?"

"You say play host. I say lured his victim," Sir Elmer countered, unwilling to back down. "Don't act high and mighty with me, Miss Laurent. Half the papers in Europe have covered your wild antics. I fully believe you told Rex you wanted to see a friend, as you put it. It wasn't until the count showed up and Rex saw the two of you together that he realised what you'd done. Juggling two lovers in close quarters takes some cheek!"

Under other circumstances, Dora would let such accusations roll off her back. But she did no one a favour by allowing Sir Elmer to demean her in such a public manner. Quick as a bolt of lightning, she swung her hand and slapped him on his cheek.

"How dare you!" she cried.

Rex and Inga gasped in unison. They weren't the only ones. Someone else was listening and watching.

Ida Dixon marched out of Sir Elmer's bedroom with her head held high. Her cheeks were pink with anger. She showed no sign of sympathy for the perfect handprint emblazoned on Sir Elmer's face. "Elmer! Is this how you treat a lady? You know Miss Laurent is one of my idols!"

Sir Elmer shrank under his companion's angry glare. "Come now, Ida. I was upset..."

His contrition caused Ida to soften her stance. "I know, darling. You've been at sixes and sevens since we came upstairs." She stroked his cheek where it still flamed, and then looked at Dora. "You must forgive him, Miss Laurent. He's taken the count's death hard."

Dora lifted her head to show she was unbowed. Before she could reply, the count's bedroom door reopened. Harris stood in the doorway and glowered at the group.

"What's all this?" he asked. "I heard shouting. Who are you?"

Sir Elmer offered his hand. "Sir Elmer Holmes. The count is... was one of my closest friends."

"Was is right," Harris replied. "He's no one's friend now. But since you're here, you can tell me all about him."

Dora wasn't about to be left out. She shifted into the role of hostess and took control of the proceedings. "Let's all go to the drawing room. Between Sir Elmer and myself, I'm sure we can answer most of your questions about the life of Count Vasile Zugravescu."

Chapter 10
Police browbeating

Rex never failed to be amazed at Dora's abilities to manoeuvre the people around her. In a matter of minutes, she'd taken Sir Elmer from an angry accuser to an apologetic guest. The only shame was that Benedict hadn't been there to witness the transformation.

The drawing room fire still roared. Dora asked Percival to see to tea and sandwiches for the group.

"This isn't a tea party," Harris said, glaring at Dora.

"It most certainly isn't," she agreed, holding her own. "But many of us skipped dinner, and I imagine this won't be short. Light refreshments will ensure everyone's good humour. Including yours, Constable Harris."

"Fine," he grumbled. He motioned for everyone to take a seat before claiming the dowager's wingback for himself.

Rex sincerely hoped his grandmother didn't make an appearance. While he trusted her to go along with Harris's sudden change in role, he didn't want to see her face if she saw Harris lounging in her chair.

The tea and refreshments arrived in short order. Percival poured steaming cups for each of them. Despite his earlier grumblings, Harris helped himself to one of each of the sandwiches on offer. He ate two in rapid fashion, reminding Rex that due to his request for help, Harris likely hadn't eaten supper.

Temporarily sated, Harris pulled a stenography pad and pen from his coat pocket and looked up expectantly. "Which one of you wants to start?"

Rex glanced between Dora and Sir Elmer.

Dora inclined her head in Sir Elmer's direction. "If we're going to begin at the beginning, then you should speak first. You knew him longer than I did."

Ida snuggled closer to Sir Elmer on the sofa they had chosen. The two of them sat to Harris's right, while Dora and Rex occupied the space to his left.

Sir Elmer cleared his throat and began. "I met Vasile seven years ago, while stationed in France, like most men my age. Unlike Lord Rex, I was a low-ranking enlisted man, but I gained a reputation for my fierceness on the battlefield and seeming invincibility. I was one of the few who'd say yes when assigned what was likely to be a suicide mission."

"I take it you met the count on one of these death missions?"

"Yes, indeed. The sergeant called me in and introduced the count as Vasile — no title or surname — and said he needed my help to sneak past the enemy lines. We took off the next day, leaving before dawn. Around noon, a baby's cry caught my ear."

"A baby? So close to the front line?" Dora asked.

"Practically a newborn," he said with a grimace. "We crept closer and saw a pair of women — grandmother, mother, and baby — huddled in front of a farmhouse. Half a dozen Huns held them at gunpoint. I'd been at the front to guess at the sad ending in store. This time, I was determined to do something to stop it. I told Vasile to hide in the woods. I'd come back for him after I rescued the family."

Harris leaned forward, caught up in the tale. "Did he stay behind? Did you save them?"

"Six against one was a death sentence. Vasile argued with me, but I was immoveable. We were there to defend women and children. When I said that, he caved. He provided cover while I got into place. He took out three of the enemy before they knew what was happening. I got two more, although it was a close thing. The older woman in the bunch struck the remaining German with a shovel. When word reached camp of our bravery, as told by the grateful family, I received a promotion. It was the first of the commendations that led to me eventually receiving a knighthood from the king."

"What about Vasile?" Rex asked. "Did he ever explain why he needed to cross enemy lines?"

"Vasile stayed tightlipped about the reason for that mission. After the war ended, and we ran into one another at an event, I found out he had a title and a connection to his country's royal family."

Harris scowled at his notes. "Why would a member of the royal family, distant or otherwise, be running around the war front on his own?"

"I'm sure he had his reasons," Sir Elmer replied. "My guess is that he acted as some kind of messenger. Read into that what you will."

Harris wrote the information on his pad. "What about you, Miss Laurent? When did you make the count's acquaintance?"

"Nearly four years ago. I was in Nice, enjoying the seaside by day and casino by night. Vasile slid into place beside me at the card table and whispered advice into my ear. He told me to fold, but I ignored him, and won the pot. Afterwards, he offered to buy me a drink in exchange for knowing why I'd felt confident enough to play my hand." Dora's voice grew wistful. She pretended to be lost in her recollections. "We bumped into one another again the next night, that time on a dinner cruise. After the third night in a row, we decided fate was sending us a message. We were destined to be friends. And so we were."

"Friends?" Sir Elmer arched an eyebrow.

Dora flicked her wrist, tossing aside his emphasis on semantics. "Vasile and I made no promises. There are few men who can keep up with me, Sir Elmer. Vasile made a good run of it when we first met. Lord Rex is proving to have more staying power. I repeat, there was no reason for Rex to be jealous of Vasile, nor vice versa."

"What's this now?" Harris said, intervening before Dora and Sir Elmer could get into another spat. "Jealousy, huh? Sir Elmer, you think that is the motive?"

Sir Elmer shrugged. "I can think of no other."

Harris pretended to contemplate Sir Elmer's suggestion. Rex's shoulders tightened. Even knowing Harris wasn't a real officer did little to assuage his anxiety anytime he found himself staring at the noose.

Harris allowed the silence to stretch until all four people facing him leaned forward in their seats. Finally, he shook his head. "No, I can't see it. That doesn't fit with the crime scene."

Sir Elmer stared agog at Harris. "What you mean doesn't fit? I wasn't aware that jealous murderers had a preferred method of attack."

"That's where you're wrong, sir. The means of death is usually an excellent indicator of the motive for the crime. Take death by poisoning, for example. In most cases, the decline happens slowly, stretching over days and weeks. This makes them awfully hard to detect. Nine times out of ten, the culprit is a woman. Women have access to the food, and patience in spades."

Sir Elmer crossed his arms and gazed at Harris with something approaching respect.

Rex took advantage of Sir Elmer's changing opinion to nudge Harris along. "You made your point well, Constable. You examined the scene. What does your experienced eye suggest happened?"

"Before I begin, allow me to paint the picture for those of you who didn't enter the room. First, there were no signs that the count had invited anyone else into the room. There was a single glass on the nightstand, still half-full of water. The count hadn't bothered to unpack. He'd stripped to his undershirt, tossed his clothes on a nearby chair, and climbed into bed. On the other half of the bed, the covers were not rumpled. From what I can see, the murderer struck while he was asleep. I don't suppose any of you know why he was so tired?"

Dora spoke up. "He'd had an awful journey getting here and plead exhaustion shortly after he arrived. I poured him a finger of whiskey to help take the edge off. He stayed long enough to drink it and then excused himself."

"That explains the faint scent of alcohol I noted when I went near him," Harris replied. He made more notes on his pad.

Sir Elmer cleared his throat to get Harris's attention. "So the man was abed alone. I fail to see how this excludes Lord Rex from consideration. The count told him of his plans to nap. Lord Rex had the keys, and plenty of time between the arrival of his guests and the dinner bell. Why are you so certain?"

Harris eyed the man and motioned with his hand. "It's obvious!"

"Perhaps to one as well-versed in crime as you are, Constable. I'm afraid you're going to have to spell it out for the rest of us."

Harris rubbed his forehead. "Let me try a different approach, one where we assume you are correct. The story begins with Lord Rex inviting someone he considered to be an arch-rival for his companion's affections into his home. The men meet for the first time and engage in a brief conversation with Miss Laurent in the room. Thus far, no one has said anything about the men raising their voices or having a scuffle. The count takes his leave and goes to sleep. Yet, you'd have us believe that Lord Rex let himself into the count's bedroom, where he stabbed the sleeping man in his back?"

Harris stopped to make sure everyone was paying attention to what he said next. "Now, I don't know Lord Rex anymore than I know you, Sir Elmer. But I imagine that if I delve into his background, I will find he also spent time at war and earned his share of commendations. If this were a shooting at dawn, I might believe it. Instead, we've got a cold-blooded murder of someone incapacitated. I ask, would a man like yourselves commit the crime that I've outlined? It would be an incredibly cowardly and dishonourable thing to do."

Sir Elmer harrumphed, but he didn't voice any disagreement. In a few sentences, Harris had poked so many holes in Sir Elmer's suspicions that they could no longer hold water. Rex's spirits rose.

"Well then, Constable! Since you are so clever, who is the killer?" Sir Elmer asked, still with his knickers in a twist.

Harris barked a laugh in reply. "If solving murders were that easy, they'd have no need of men like me. As far as I'm concerned, you are all suspects, both guests and staff alike. I will need to speak with everyone to get a full accounting of their time in the last twelve hours."

"Everyone?" Ida cried. "Oh Elmer, I don't like this. I don't want to stay in a house with a murderer, no matter how grand it is."

Sir Elmer's face flushed as he grasped what Harris was saying. "You can't possibly think we are to blame. Count Vasile was one of my dearest friends. I'd have absolutely no reason whatsoever to want him dead. If I could go back in time and save him, I would."

Harris raised his eyebrows and nodded at Miss Dixon. "And what of her? Are you as certain of her innocence?"

"Me?" Ida screeched. "I'd never even met the man. I'd never met anyone here before."

"So you claim." Harris said blandly, eliciting another shriek from Ms Dixon. "Until I can be certain of that fact, no one is going anywhere."

Sir Elmer was bristling with rage, but he visibly fought for calm. Flying off the handle right now, in front of the Constable, was the worst thing he could do.

Sensing the moment of danger had passed, Harris shifted in his chair to face Rex. "I want to make a proper inventory of the room, but I won't be able to get more officers out here until morning. Do you have somewhere we can store the body overnight?"

Rex blanched. Store the body? He had given no thought to moving the count from his current resting place. However, the expression on Harris's face clarified that wasn't an option. Now that it was on his mind, Rex didn't savour the idea of sleeping down the hall from a corpse.

He got up and crossed the room, where he pulled the cord to call the help. "I have no idea, Constable, but if anyone can find a place, it will be our butler, Percival."

Chapter 11
Dora pulls back the curtain

Dora tossed and turned for most of the night, her dreams plagued by memories of her time with Count Vasile. Around two in the morning, she gave up any pretence of rest. After stoking the coals in the fire, she settled into her meditative position on the floor and closed her eyes. She inhaled and exhaled until her thoughts settled.

She'd told Sir Elmer the truth about how she'd met Vasile. What she hadn't mentioned is those casual encounters had been nothing of the sort. Vasile had targeted her. She'd been the object of his attention, but not his affection.

From the moment she laid eyes on him, he'd seemed too good to be true. He was so suave and debonair, yet he treated her as though she were the one who walked on water. Vasile smoothed over her concerns, providing an answer or explanation for everything. For that reason, it took her a while to see past his facade.

By then, she'd spent several weeks at his beck and call, letting him sweep her off her feet when it was convenient for him, and set her aside when he had other obligations. He silenced her concerns with a flurry of kisses and caresses.

It took her nearly a month to notice that Inga didn't like him. Inga never said a word against him, but the truth lay in her searching glances when she thought Dora wasn't paying attention. Then word came from Lord Audley of a new assignment. They had to move on.

Dora found herself split in two. Her heart and mind said she had to stick to her chosen path of being a spy. Her soul cried at the thought of leaving Vasile behind. Dora went to Inga for advice. Inga answered her question with another.

"Before you talk to him, answer me this. Why did you feel the need to come to me for guidance? You've never hesitated on a decision before. Why now?"

That stumped Dora. It took some deep soul-searching to uncover the reason. She feared he'd say no. She stopped talking and started paying closer attention whenever he was around. It was only then that she caught sight of the expressions he worked so hard to keep hidden from her. The forced smiles. The ardent promises of unending love that didn't reach his eyes.

In the end, she resorted to what she did best to find out the truth. Vasile had cancelled their plans at the last minute, leaving her with nothing to do. So she'd dressed in men's clothing and ventured to his hotel. The door to his balcony stood open, and the light was on in his room. A trellis of bougainvillea offered the possibility to get close enough to see and hear inside. She pulled on her gloves and took care to watch for thorns. Under the cover of darkness, she blended into the shadows cast by the balcony.

Vasile was inside, deep in conversation with his valet while he dressed for a night out, instead of being under the covers with a head cold. Dora had choked back her sob before it could give her away. But the tears ran freely while she listened in.

"Any luck with the room searches, Luca?" Vasile asked. A muffled 'no' answered him. He groaned in frustration. "That's the end, then. We'll have to report back that there is no truth to the rumours of a new British spy."

Out of sight, Dora's hair stood on end and a shiver wracked her spine. She gripped tight onto the trellis to keep from falling.

"What of your arm candy? You've spent more nights with Miss Laurent than away from her. Have you finally fallen under someone's spell?"

Vasile's laugh boomed through the air and cut through Dora's heart with the sharpness of a sword. "I admit she's cleverer than most and easy on the eyes, but it will take more than that to tempt me from my course. I should send her a thank you gift before we go, however. She provided the perfect cover for me. With her on my arm, I was the dashing Romanian count living a playboy life. People openly whispered their secrets even though I was within earshot. No one feared me."

Vasile laughed again, his valet joining in. Dora didn't need to hear another word. She wanted to be out of there, away from Nice and Vasile and his empty promises. Tears blurred her vision and her throat burned as she held back a sob. In her rush to get away, her hand slipped. She'd swung sideways and earned a deep scratch across her inner thigh before she found a new grip.

The pain spiked up into her groin and gave her a moment of clarity. She didn't want to be caught there, red-eyed, bleeding, and lurking in the shadows. She sucked in a deep breath, begged her heart to slow, and methodically made her way down.

Inga was waiting in her room when she made it back. Her dear friend said not a single word of condemnation while she cleaned Dora's wound. Inga didn't break her silence until she'd tucked Dora into bed.

"Try, fail, learn, and try again. This is our motto, Dora. You tried your hand at love, and you failed because of his choices, not yours. Mourn tonight, but come sunrise, I want you to move on to learning. You fell prey to a master because you are not experienced enough right now. While the scars on your heart and leg heal, consider what you can take away from his methods."

Dora knew how to pick herself up, and how to rise to any challenge set forth for her. She leaned upon that strength to keep a straight face when Vasile came to say goodbye. She accepted the diamond brooch he offered, and never gave a hint that she was anything other than sorry to bid him adieu.

She and Inga moved on. By the time she met Vasile again, she was older, wiser, and much more worldly. She laughed, flirted, and waltzed around him, always remaining one step out of reach. As far as Dora knew, Vasile never found out just how close he'd come to unmasking the secret British spy.

Never again had Dora allowed her heart to drive her decisions. Until now, that was. All those hours with Rex, watching him grow and progress. Was it any wonder he'd got under her skin?

The pink chiffon monstrosity hung in the corner of her room. She opened her eyes and looked upon it. That was the kind of girl Rex needed... the kind he deserved. Someone who would fawn over him, and think him the greatest man in the world.

Someone who was like she'd been four years earlier when she met Count Vasile for the first time.

But that wasn't her anymore. She'd balked at the dress when she'd opened the box, and her instinctual reaction hadn't changed in the days since.

Inga was wrong. Having a fling with Rex so she could get it out of her system was not the answer. It was, in fact, the very worst thing she could do to them both.

As Marcus Tullius Cicero more elegantly put it, "Any man can make mistakes, but only an idiot persists in his error."

This time around, Dora was in the count's proverbial shoes. She'd be the one waving goodbye, leaving Rex to reassemble the shattered pieces of his heart. But only if she persisted along a path she knew was incorrect.

For better or worse, Vasile taught her that they walked a lonely road. Yes, trusted friends guarded their back. But no one stood at their side.

Dora needed to keep it that way, no matter how much that decision hurt.

She closed her eyes again, sat still with her decision, and breathed in and out until she found her resolve. Finally, the languor of sleep tugged her back to her bed. Alone, under the covers, she shivered until she drifted into a dreamless slumber.

* * *

By the time she finally arose, it was long after the first hints of dawn seeped from beneath the curtains. Her head was clear of the fog that had clouded her thoughts the night before. Clarity was going to be much in demand, given her assignment for the day.

After a light knock on the door, her friend Inga walked in. "Rise and shine, dear. We've got a long day ahead of us. Harris left before dawn."

"Where did he go?"

"To gather his officers. Audley is sending a few trustworthy men in his employ. Harris is waiting for them at the old farmhouse up the road. He wants to make sure they're up to snuff before he brings them to the house."

"Where he'll assign them guard duties over the exits. Yes, now I remember." Dora splashed her face with water from her basin and patted it dry. "Has Rex spoken with Lord and Lady Lambert?"

"I doubt you were the only one who remained awake last night. Everyone chose to lie in this morning. Like a lion awaiting its prey, Rex is staking out the breakfast room."

"In that case, I'll ring for a tray. I have no desire to butt heads with that woman again this morning."

"You might want to get dressed and take your breakfast on the terrace," Inga suggested. "I spotted Mrs Murphy sneak out there with a steaming cup of coffee."

Speaking with Gladys Murphy was at the top of Dora's To Do list. She and Rex had divvied up the guests the night before. It hadn't required much thought, given Lady Lambert's total disdain for Dora.

Dora had enjoyed her walk with Mrs Murphy the day before. Gladys was a woman out of her depth, suddenly thrust into the world of politics and high society. Dora had the urge to take her under her wing. With a little training, she'd be an excellent asset to her rising star of a husband.

Dora dashed into her dressing room and grabbed a pair of wool, wide-leg trousers, a thin silk blouse, and an autumnal maroon sweater coat that belted at her waist. Her selection was entirely based on what was the fastest to pull on. Inga helped with hair and a thin line of kohl around her eyes. After a sweep of red lipstick, she was ready to go.

Before she left the room, she turned back with a question. "I forgot to ask. What are you doing today?"

"I'm tasked with consulting our walking encyclopaedia of society gossip to glean what I can about our guests."

Dora rolled her eyes at Inga's grandiose choice of words. "You're spending the day with Edith?"

"Got it in one. Now hurry. You don't want to miss Mrs Murphy."

Dora opted for the back stairs out of a lack of desire to bump into anyone else. A housemaid stood near the terrace doorway, keeping watch over Mrs Murphy, ready to meet her every need. Dora put in a request for a light repast and then headed outside to join her guest.

Gladys tossed a worried glance over her shoulder when Dora opened the door. Her gaze softened when she saw who it was.

"Fear not. It is I, and not Lady Lambert," Dora declared. Her bold words coaxed a grin from Gladys.

"I hate to be uncharitable, but I cannot imagine why anyone would invite her into their home."

Dora grinned back at Gladys, although her mouth had a decidedly sly slant to it. "Women of her ilk only strike those below. I take heart from knowing I am above them in all ways that truly count, despite what they might think."

"Wise words," Gladys replied. "Especially for someone so young. Yet, I notice you are outside with me, rather than enjoying the warmth of the breakfast room."

"I find myself in need of spiritual warmth, rather than physical heat. Nothing fills the soul better than the brisk morning air and this unparalleled view of the Cotswolds."

The ground sloped away, offering a sweeping view over the gardens and beyond. The undulating hills, with their patchwork layout, imbued viewers with a sense of tranquillity. Dry stone walls formed barriers between the fields and furrowed lands. A copse of trees marked the edge of the lake. Although Dora couldn't spy the village of Ducklington from where she stood, it wasn't far away. If Lady Lambert carried on with haranguing everyone, Dora would propose they nip out to the local for a pint and a basket of chips.

The maid returned, bearing a tray of food and drink. There was more than enough for both of them. Dora held out her hands for a warm cup of milky coffee. She sipped it while the maid laid out the plates and food.

"Would you care to join me?" Dora asked Gladys, once all was arranged.

"Yes, thank you. I wasn't hungry when I first came out, but the fresh air has awakened my appetite."

They chose seats at the square table set out for that exact purpose. Laid with a tablecloth, fine china, and a centrepiece of flowers, it was no different from what they'd have found inside. Dora bided her time until they'd both made headway into the breakfast foods before beginning her questioning.

"Murphy, that's an Irish surname, correct? When I saw your names on the list, I assumed you were both from the Emerald Isle, yet neither of you speaks with an accent."

"We're first generation. Our parents grew up on farms in Ireland, but left to find work. We were born here and studied at English schools where we mastered the local accent. However, put us in an Irish pub and we blend in like natives."

"From the way you speak, I take it you've known Mr Murphy for a long while."

"The Irish community is a close-knit group. We grew up in Birmingham and saw one another at parties and weddings. Our parents take credit for our match, but the truth is, we'd been eyeing one another for a long time before they took notice."

Dora clapped her hands to her chest. "A love match! Those are a rarity and are certainly to be envied. Did your husband always want to go into politics?"

Gladys frowned and shook her head. "Far from it! He was a leader within our community, but he had his gaze firmly fixed on local issues... until two years ago when home rule turned from dream to reality. Jack recognised the need for people who understood what it means to be Irish to sit in Westminster."

Dora scrunched her brow and pretended not to understand. "Home rule gave the Irish the right to decide matters on their own, right?"

"Yes, for better and worse. Our country is split into two, and our tempers are too fiery to give me hope the separation will be peaceful. The men in Westminster have the power to provide support or pull it away. Jack is now well-positioned to have a voice in deciding such matters."

"I see," Dora said. She helped herself to another slice of toast to buy herself time to determine her next move.

Much of what Gladys was telling her was not news. Lord Audley's network had uncovered most of the Murphy's background. Dora knew Jack owed his election to being in the right place at the right time. The Irish community was large enough in his area to swing the vote, particularly with such a short run-up to the election. Jack's local name recognition catapulted him to the top of the candidate list.

What was less clear was whether Jack Murphy identified as an Englishman or an Irishman living outside his true home. Gladys's answers did little to cast light over the matter. Dora was no closer to determining whether this information was even relevant. As far as she was aware, Count Vasile had nothing to do with the Irish state.

There was nothing for it. She was going to have to ask more pointed questions.

"I hope I'm not intruding, but did you and your husband know Count Vasile well? It was he who suggested we extend the invitation."

"Honestly? I'd say we were acquaintances, at best. We were surprised to receive the invite — pleasantly surprised, I mean." She flushed in embarrassment.

Dora flashed her a friendly smile. "I made sure Rex mentioned the count when he sent his note to you. Given we are strangers, I feared you wouldn't come unless you had some idea why we extended the offer."

"We'd have come in any case. After all, how often does one

get the chance to spend a weekend in a home like this?" Gladys waved her hand at the stone facade of the rear of the building. "But knowing the count would be in attendance was a bonus. We'd met him a few months earlier. He and Jack discovered a shared interest in whiskey exports. They'd made mention of exploring business opportunities. When we came home and got caught up in the election craze, all thoughts of anything else fell to the wayside."

"So you believe the count included you because he wanted to further these business discussions?"

Gladys shrugged. "That's my best guess. You'll think this an exaggeration, but this is the first time we've put our feet up since Jack was pressed into running for office. In London, Jack would have most certainly struggled to find time to fit the count into his busy schedule. Here, time is just one luxury Ducklington Manor offers."

Dora kept her face blank, but her stomach soured. Time was not her friend, not with the count's body cooling in a storeroom. The estate's hold on its charms would loosen once Harris returned with the guards. Ducklington Manor would become a temporary, highly gilded prison, until Dora and Rex identified the count's killer and their motivations.

Gladys dabbed her mouth with her napkin. "I should go upstairs and begin packing."

"Packing?" Dora grimaced. "I assumed Rex sent word."

"No, I've not seen him today. Perhaps he spoke with Jack? My husband got up early and set off for a walk. Said he wanted to make the most of the peace and quiet."

"The police constable arrived late last night. He's declared no one can leave until he finishes his investigation. I expect he'll return any minute now with his officers."

Gladys's smile wobbled. "I see. Of course, that makes

sense." She settled back into her chair and reached for her coffee.

"You took that news well," Dora said.

"I can't say it is a total surprise. I'd hoped we might slip away before the news hounds get word of Jack's presence. At least if we're all cooped up here, there's less risk of the news getting out."

"You're not worried about what the Constable may find?"

Gladys scoffed. "As I said, Theodora, we barely knew the count. His death is terrible, don't get me wrong, but we have nothing to fear from an investigation."

When Gladys finally took her leave, Dora remained outside in the sun. To anyone walking past, she appeared to be admiring the view. In reality, she was deep in thought.

Gladys was a cool character... maybe too cool. Dora had so little to go on that she couldn't decide whether it was fatalism guiding the woman's reaction or an excellent acting job.

Chapter 12
Rex makes inquiries

R ex folded the paper and laid it beside his plate. He'd read
the daily news front to back twice already while waiting
for Lord and Lady Lambert to put in an appearance at
breakfast. Short of sending up a housemaid to rouse them,
which was absolutely out of the question, he needed to find a
way to occupy himself for a while longer.

He gave the breakfast room a slow scan, taking time to
admire the changes his grandmother had recently made. While
she'd seen no need to update the interiors of the main rooms in
Ducklington Manor, she'd made an exception for the breakfast
room.

Located in the rear of the house, with a southerly facing
view, it was well placed to take full advantage of the morning
sun. For this reason, the dowager had hired an architect to
replace the straight rear wall with an expansive bow front lined
with bay windows. From where he sat, Rex enjoyed an almost
one hundred and eighty degree view of the rolling Cotswold
hills.

He knew the layout of those hills as well as he knew the
back of his hand. That first rise had been where he and his

brother arranged archery tournaments for visiting children. If he gazed at it for too long, he'd lose himself in his childhood recollections. While that might be fine on any other day, this morning Rex had higher priorities.

Rex forced his gaze away from the outdoors and instead looked at the people in the room. Unlike in the dining room, his grandmother had furnished this area with a collection of five smaller square tables. She said that breakfast was a time people often liked to be alone, especially after playing games late the night before. The small tables prevented the need for unwelcome small talk while still enabling groups of four.

Sir Elmer, for example, took full advantage of the space in the room. He bid a perfunctory good morning to Rex, and then settled himself at the table closest to the window. If that hadn't been evidence enough of his desire for silence, he soon opened the newspapers and spread them in front of himself. Other than a periodic grunt or grumble, he had not said another word.

Nonetheless, Rex had been sorry to see him leave. Inga was off, rousing Dora from bed. Harris was rounding up his patrol. He'd run into Patrick Murphy on his way down, but the man had declared his need to stretch his legs. As for his grandmother, Mrs Murphy, and Miss Dixon, there was no sign of them. In all likelihood, they were taking breakfast in their room.

Now he was on his own, if one excluded the footmen standing against the wall. The twins, Archie and Basel, stood in the middle of the line, looking like a pair of finely matched candlesticks. If they were in London, Rex would have invited them to join him. But here, with strangers in their midst, Rex didn't dare to do anything that might hint at his friendship with the staff.

Instead, Rex noticed how well the two London men fitted in with the rest of the servants. In their matching house uniforms, one would never guess that as recently as six months earlier, the two had been living in one of the most dangerous areas of London. Theirs was just one transformation that Dora had overseen since her arrival in London.

Did his grandmother look at him with the same awe? She'd had a front-row seat to his progress from restless young lord to professional spy. His grandmother must have noticed the changes from his months of training. Rex made a note to ask her at the next opportunity.

Rex spent another quarter hour dawdling. Then, he started guessing where the artwork on the wall came from. When Benedict Cavendish walked in, Rex was ready to fall to his knees and give thanks. However, he reined in the impulse and waved for Benedict to join him.

Rex had somehow forgotten Dora's brother was there. Given a corpse in his cellars, he forgave himself. He refilled his cup of tea while Benedict helped himself to the breakfast buffet. When the man took the seat opposite him, he struck up a genial conversation.

"Good morning, Lord Benedict. Did you sleep well?"

Benedict's knife scratched across his plate. "Did I sleep well? With everything going on?"

"Err, well, yes?" Rex cleared his throat. "You are the only guest with nothing to fear. If you didn't sleep well, what hope is there for the rest of us?"

Benedict resumed cutting his slice of bacon. "I suppose that is true. It wasn't the best night of sleep I've experienced, but that wasn't due to any fault with the room. What of you, Lord Rex? Was everything handled as expected?"

Benedict's emphasis on the word made clear his question.

"The local constable arrived to take control of the situation. He'll be back this morning to begin his interviews. Unfortunately, no one may leave until he is satisfied he's identified the killer."

Benedict shuddered at Rex's blunt words. He abandoned his serving of scrambled eggs and opted for dry toast instead. "If I can be of assistance, please don't hesitate to call upon me."

"Thank you. I mean that. For the moment, there's little to do but find ways to amuse ourselves. However, should things change, I will let you know."

Benedict inclined his head in a silent acknowledgment. The men fell into a comfortable silence, each occupied with his thoughts.

The door swung open, and Lord Lambert finally put in an appearance. He was suitably attired for a weekend in the countryside, wearing a tweed suit and an open collar shirt. His face, however, displayed evidence of a rough night of sleep. Lord Lambert scanned the room and flushed when he saw Rex and Benedict.

After all his time waiting, Rex wasn't taking any chances that Lord Lambert might sit elsewhere. He hailed the man. "Lord Lambert, come sit with us. We've space aplenty and the morning papers."

Lord Lambert shuffled over and took the seat to Rex's right. "Lord Rex, I'm pleased to see you harbour no ill will toward myself after yesterday evening. My wife was upset by the news and spoke without thinking."

Rex didn't agree with all of Lord Lambert's assessment of his wife's behaviour, but now wasn't the time to be pedantic. He needed Lord Lambert's good will to last long enough for him to gather information.

Rex brushed the unspoken apology aside. "Emotions were charged, Lord Lambert, which is certainly understandable given the circumstances. Let's not speak of it again. How is Lady Lambert this morning?"

Lord Lambert gave Rex an apologetic smile. "I checked on her before coming down. She claims to have a headache, but she was sitting up in bed with a cup of hot chocolate and a plate of croissants."

"Avoiding the rest of us. I can't say I blame her. The weekend is certainly not going as planned." Rex shook his head in consternation. "But we will keep a stiff upper lip and carry on, as one must. Please, help yourself to some food. The sausages are from the village."

Benedict excused himself then. "I need to make a telephone call and then I thought I'd take advantage of your library, if that's all right."

"Of course. Make yourself at home," Rex replied. Although Rex would never have encouraged Benedict to leave, he was grateful to have time along with Lord Lambert. The man was more likely to be forthcoming if no one else was there to listen in.

Like Benedict, Lord Lambert opted for the traditional English fare of eggs, sausage, beans, mushrooms, and toast. Despite the ordinary names of the dishes, the cook prepared each one to exacting specifications, using herbs from the garden and local meats. Lord Lambert dug into his meal with gusto.

Rex waited for him to come up for air, as it was. He filled the gap by prattling on about the local game and fisheries. Lord Lambert nodded along at the appropriate points, all the while devouring his meal. When at last his plate was clean, he wiped the corners of his mouth and gave Rex a downcast expression.

"I'd been so looking forward to hunting this weekend. But, what with all that has happened, I imagine such pursuits are no longer feasible."

"I'm afraid you might be right. However, the constable is due shortly. He intends to speak with everyone and has already said that no one is to leave until he has solved the case. Perhaps he'll be amenable to allowing us some form of entertainment, given we're basically trapped."

"Lillian won't be happy to hear that news," Lord Lambert groaned. "But your grandmother is here now. She, at least, is a suitable companion. No offence to your young woman," he hastened to add.

"Theodora has never let societal lines restrict her opportunities to befriend someone. Case in point is my grandmother. I wouldn't be at all surprised if Lady Lambert is singing a different tune before it is time for you to leave."

"For the sake of all of us, I do hope you're right. Since we're being so honest, I'll admit I'd have much preferred you invited us a different weekend. Most of the guests are strangers to us. Beyond you and your grandmother, only Sir Elmer's face was familiar."

Rex frowned. "And Count Vasile. Surely you count him as a friend."

"No," Lord Lambert said with no hesitation. "Never met the man before in my life. Or his life, I should say. Now, we never will."

Rex rocked back in his chair. Lord Lambert's words made no sense. Despite the clarity of them, Rex must have misunderstood.

"Count Vasile specifically requested your presence. It was exactly as we said last night. Theodora invited the count here and offered to add to the guest list anyone else he was hoping to see. He provided your names, Sir Elmer, and the Murphys. My grandmother and Lord Benedict were last-minute additions."

"What you say makes no sense, old boy. Sir Elmer and the count were clearly chums. I can't speak for the Murphys, but I assure you, I didn't know the man from Adam. I couldn't even describe him!"

This news flabbergasted Rex. He wished that he and Dora had swapped places, and that he'd taken the assignment to speak with the Murphys. Surely she'd do a better job of dealing with this announcement.

What else could Rex do but muddle through and gather as much information as possible? "I am as perplexed as you, sir. Can you think of any reason Count Vasile would want you here? Perhaps a shared acquaintance?"

Lord Lambert shook his head. "Best as I can see, the only connection we have in common is you. Or rather, your beautiful companion."

"But surely there must be a reason," Rex insisted. "Have you recently made any new investments, or expressed interest in exploring new options? Or what of Lady Lambert? Has she any connections to Europe?"

"Lady Lambert's only European relationship is with her couturier in Paris. Given the size of her dress bills, I'd prefer that connection diminish, not grow. As for the rest, you'd have to ask my man who oversees my business affairs. I don't dirty my hands, if you know what I mean."

Rex searched for another angle to explore, but came up short. Whatever reason Count Vasile held for wanting to meet Lord Lambert would forever be a secret.

Unless there was something in the count's bags to give them a clue.

Percival entered the breakfast room and came straight to Rex. "The Constable has arrived, my lord. He's asked to speak with you before he begins his interrogations."

"Show him to the library, Percival. I'll be there in a minute."

Percival gave a polite cough. "I believe Lord Benedict is currently occupying that space."

How had Rex forgotten about the man again? But he had asked to be involved. No better place to start than the beginning.

"Lord Benedict is welcome to remain, if he so chooses. He

can be among the first to take his turn with the constable. If you don't mind, could you send word of the constable's arrival to Miss Laurent?"

"Of course, my lord. I already took the liberty of sending a housemaid to find her."

Lord Lambert laid claim to the newspaper. "I'll stay out of the way for now, if it's all the same to you."

"Wise man," Rex replied. "What I'd give to do the same. Duty calls."

Duty and an inordinate amount of curiosity. Rex could hardly wait to see how the others would react to the news about the Lamberts. He suspected a dead body wasn't the only surprise in store for them this weekend.

Chapter 13
The guessing game

After Archie alerted Dora about Harris's arrival, she hurried across the house to join the others in the library. So intent was she upon her task that she didn't notice the broad-shouldered man stepping out of the alcove until it was too late.

"Oof!" she grunted when she caught an elbow in her side. "I'm so sorry. I didn't see you there."

The man in question straightened up and turned around, giving her a clear view of his face. Of all people, it had to be Benedict. Had he been lying in wait for her? "What are you doing here?" she hissed.

"I was making a telephone call, if you must know," her brother replied in a snooty voice.

Given it was a weekend, Dora could not imagine whom Benedict rang. He didn't have a wife and children waiting for him back home... only their parents. That line of thought led her to the obvious conclusion.

"You called your father?" she asked, choosing her phrasing carefully.

Benedict refused to answer. He marched off toward the library without a backward glance. Dora was having none of it.

After a quick look around to make sure no one stood within hearing distance, she grabbed the back of his coat and pulled.

He jerked backwards, just as she had intended.

"Why, pray tell, did you ring the Duke?"

Benedict avoided meeting her gaze, showing no signs of willingness to confess. Dora gave the back of his jacket another ruthless tug.

"Will you stop doing that?" he sniped. "You're going to leave wrinkles in the fabric."

"Wrinkles in the fabric are going to be the least of your worries if you don't come clean about what you are doing."

"Fine," he spat. "Given the seriousness of the situation, yes, I sought guidance from my father."

Interesting. Dora would have given a pound coin to have been an eavesdropper on the line for that conversation. "And? Did he advise you to pack your bag and run home?"

Benedict's expression soured. "No, he told me to trust the process. Whatever that means."

Dora was powerless against the laughter that bubbled up inside of her. She continued to snicker as they walked into the library.

Rex and Harris sat in the small sitting area near the fireplace. Dora was more intrigued by the three men standing near the windows. Benedict's gaze followed hers, and Dora could have sworn she spotted a flash of relief cross his face.

"There you are," said Harris. "Is Inga joining us?"

"She's busy consulting the oracle in the upstairs sitting room," Dora answered.

Harris wrinkled his brow for a moment until he realised who she meant. "That was wise of her. I'll make a note to check with her later to see what she learned. In the meantime, allow me to introduce you to my officers."

He motioned for the three men to come closer. Dora

recognised each of them from her years of meetings with Lord Audley. She'd seen them take on various identities, from footmen to drivers to clerical staff. They were the perfect choice to lend a hand with their current predicament. Silent, strong, and incorruptible.

"Smith, Everly, and Higgins will act as security around the house," Harris explained, indicating each man. "I plan to station one at the front, one at the rear, and one below stairs, unless someone has a better recommendation." When no one answered, he continued, "I've got a fourth man keeping watch over the turn into the drive, and a final man stationed in the village. Although it is far more likely we'll find the murderer among our guests, I wanted to cover every possibility. Especially because we need to give the appearance of conducting a full investigation."

"You are the expert, Harris. Do whatever you think is right," Dora said.

With Dora's approval, Harris dispatched the men to their assigned places. He waited until the library door was once again firmly shut before explaining what else he had in store. "Obviously, I'll need to speak with each of the guests. However, before we do that, I want to touch on the topic of the murder weapon. Did any of you recognise it?"

"It was a sixteenth century dagger, allegedly a spoil of war against the Spanish Armada," Dora said.

"When did you figure that out?" Rex asked.

"Did I get it wrong?"

"No, but I'm amazed that you can quote the provenance."

"Would you mind illuminating the rest of us?" Harris asked.

Rex inclined his head in Dora's direction.

Dora provided the reply. "The dagger was hanging on the wall of my bedroom, above the fireplace. I noticed it on my first night and asked Percival about it. It was part of a collection of antiques on display. I was late getting ready for dinner and so I did not spot its absence."

"You're claiming someone broke into your bedroom, took a dagger from a display, and then used it to murder the count?" Benedict asked. "That's mighty convenient for you."

"As incredulous as that seems, it is the truth." Dora had been contemplating the matter from the moment she spotted the knife sticking from Count Vasile's back. "I was out for most of the afternoon, first showing Mrs Murphy around the grounds and then accompanying Inga on an errand. I had not locked my bedroom door. Therefore, it would have been easy enough for anyone to slip inside and help themselves. They had also moved my letter opener. My guess is that our villain grabbed the first available option, but spotted a better solution on their way out of the room."

Harris rubbed his chin while he pondered over the new information. "Based on what you just said, part of me wants to believe that this was a last-minute decision on the part of our murderer. However, I can't make that square with how early in the weekend they killed the count. He'd seen no one other than the two of you," he said, pointing to Dora and Rex. "Are you sure the count didn't give away anything revealing?"

Dora and Rex exchanged another set of glances. This time Rex answered.

"Several times already, I've replayed as much of the conversation as I can remember. Nothing stands out. The Count arrived, looking somewhat dishevelled, and explained he was exhausted after a rough start to his journey. Dora poured him a glass of whiskey, and we engaged in more polite chatter while he finished his drink. As soon as he was done, he excused himself to go take a nap. That's it."

Harris crossed his arms. "That's not even worth writing down. With the murder weapon now accounted for, I'll move onto the next item on my list. The count's baggage. If you can ask one of the footmen to bring it down, we'll go through it here."

Rex rang for the footman, and Archie arrived. After explaining what they needed, Rex gave him the key to the count's bedroom door. "Lock up behind you. Not that I think anyone would, but it's best if we remove any temptation to wander in and survey the scene."

The group took a moment to help themselves to tea while they waited for Archie's return. Dora took special note of her brother during the delay. She caught him keeping a close eye on Harris. Based on his narrowed gaze, he was searching the man for some hint of his background and suitability for his current task. If one didn't know Harris well, it would be hard to square the butler with a penchant for brightly coloured fabric with the detective in the dour black suit.

Dora, however, was wise to the many facets a man could have. Within their social sphere, it was unusual to find a man willing to display his deepest thoughts and truest passions for all the world to see... and judge.

Therein lay the problem. If Benedict chose to disparage or demean Harris at any point, he'd find himself facing off against her, instead. For now, he kept his thoughts to himself.

It took two trips for Archie and another footman to bring in Vasile's luggage. He'd packed enough to last him for weeks away, storing his possessions in two large leather trunks and a smaller briefcase. Before the group could dive into the count's possessions, they had to clear space for the trunks.

It took several minutes and a third footman to shift the furniture around enough to have a wide open space in the middle of the seating area. After they departed, Dora opened the briefcase.

"Huh?" she muttered, attracting the undivided attention of everyone else in the room.

"Did you find something?" Rex asked.

"It's more a case of what I'm not finding. Other than a few half-written letters and his passport, there's nothing else here." Dora wasn't daunted yet. She ran her fingers around the edge of the case, checking for any loose seams or other indications of hidden compartments. One corner of the fabric pulled free. Her aha turned to ugh when there was nothing but an old, empty envelope underneath. "Where is his ticket for his onward journey? His money? His diary?"

"Maybe they're in his trunks?" Benedict suggested. He leaned forward to get a closer look. Dora overrode her initial temptation to block his view.

Harris flipped open the lid to the trunk nearest him and then jerked his hand back like he'd been stung. Inside lay a large swatch of deep brown fur.

"Oh, his coat! Hand it here," Dora cooed, holding her hands out. "It's pure mink with sable trim. I always envied him this piece."

Harris edged between the trunks so he could get a better view. He was as much a slave to fashion as Dora. Rex gave them a moment to appreciate the expensive coat before he cleared his throat to get their attention.

"Might we resume our search now?" he asked, with an innocent air.

"Oh yes, quite right," Harris stuttered. His pink-stained cheeks revealed his embarrassment at getting distracted at such a critical moment. He returned to the first trunk and rummaged through the contents. All he found were items of clothing.

All eyes turned to the remaining trunk. Dora, Rex, Benedict, and Harris examined the outside, searching for some hint as to whether they'd finally find what they needed. Evidence of spying, a hint as to the identity of Vasile's killer — anything at all to point them in the right direction.

Dora held up a hand. "Which trunk did they bring in first?"

"This one," Rex replied with absolute certainty. "The buckle is broken on one of the straps."

Dora scowled. Broken straps and missing contents were not what she wanted. "The trunks were stacked at the foot of Vasile's bed, right?"

"Yes," Harris and Rex confirmed in near unison.

"So, it would be a reasonable guess that this trunk, the one with the broken strap, was sitting on top. Archie and the other footman would have brought it down first and then gone back up for the one underneath."

"Yes, your logic flows as smoothly as ever." Harris unbuckled the second strap and then slid the slider button over to release the catch. Without hesitation, he flipped the lid open and stepped aside so they could all see the contents at the same time.

Unlike the other trunk, this one had a storage compartment sitting atop the clothing underneath. It was a flat tray, about three inches deep, divided into sections for easy storage of smaller items.

Once again, Dora's gaze was drawn to the vacant area. The long, rectangular space should have held his jewellery case, where he stored his collection of pocket watch fobs, tie pins, and cufflinks.

The men didn't need Dora to tell them what was missing. Harris grabbed onto the narrow leather bands looped around each end and lifted the tray free. On the right was a stack of nightshirts and underwear. On the left, a hatbox. When Harris removed the lid, there was nothing at all inside.

"Are we looking at one culprit or two?" Harris asked after a beat of contemplative silence. "Is our murderer also a thief, or did someone go into the room last night and help themselves to the count's valuables."

Dora and Rex knew better than to rush to answer Harris's rhetorical question.

Benedict, however, had less experience dealing with the unexpected twists and turns in a murder investigation. He slumped in his chair and covered his face with his hands. "Two criminals at the same house party, and my sister is playing police? It's time you all put a stop to this charade of an investigation."

Chapter 14
Another unexpected arrival

Rex shared Benedict's exasperation, even if he disagreed with the man's suggestion. A murder was bad enough, but also a robbery? The two things had to be connected.

"Let's not be hasty," he said. "We suspected Count Vasile intended to pass along a message to one of the other guests. But what if he had more than a note to share? That empty box in the trunk suggests more is missing than just a few odds and ends."

Harris put his hands on his hips. "Yes, you're right, Rex. As we can see from the other trunk, Vasile was a clothes-horse. I can't imagine him dedicating such a large space to an empty container."

Dora hazarded a guess. "What if he intended to buy something? Or pick something up? We can't preclude that as an option."

The group took some time to contemplate the implications of the empty box in the trunk. Before long, they were each tossing out ideas for what might have been inside. Eventually Dora called them to a stop.

"We could check everyone's rooms," Rex suggested.

"Too late for that, I'm afraid," Dora replied. "By now,

everyone will have unpacked. Short of repacking their trunks and cases, we have no way of figuring out whether they have more now than when they arrived."

Rex hated to admit it, but Dora was right. Investigating murders was so much easier when they could rely on Dora's favourite tactics of donning costumes and picking locks. Now, their environment worked against them. Although they had, in theory, full run of the manor, so did everyone else. They could not risk getting caught inside of someone's room.

Harris wisely chose to turn the conversation in a new direction. "I say we stick to our original plan of questioning everyone. Where should I start?"

"Not Lord and Lady Lambert," Rex said.

"Why is that?" Harris asked.

"Because, according to Lord Lambert, they had never met Count Vasile."

Dora sucked in air. "But that's preposterous! Surely you don't believe him."

"What reason had he to lie? No, seriously. Can anyone come up with an explanation for why Lord Lambert would lie about his connection with the count? I certainly cannot."

"This is going to be one of those cases where every answer we get only leads to another question," Dora muttered. "Fear not, however. Experience tells me that the questions will eventually run their course, and we'll find we have all the answers we need. There is nothing to be done but have patience."

"Or... you could call in the authorities?" Benedict offered, although everyone ignored his remark.

"Patience and hard work it is," Harris agreed. "Dora, you were supposed to speak with the Murphys this morning. Did you have better luck?"

"I did."

Rex was so pleased to hear a positive answer come from her mouth that he almost missed what she said.

"The Murphy's definitely knew Vasile, although, according to Mrs Murphy, they were little more than acquaintances. There had been talk of the possibility of a business venture or other sort of investment. I didn't get the details. The Murphys assumed that the count put them on the guest list because he wanted to further the discussions."

Rex raised to hand. "A weekend in the Cotswolds would not be my first choice of where to have a business meeting, no matter how nice the surroundings might be. Did you believe her claim?"

"Like you, I had no reason not to. She did offer justification. Mrs Murphy pointed out how busy her husband had been with the election, and how things were unlikely to settle down soon. He'll have to find a place to stay in London, hire staff, and forge friendships with his fellow party members. The life of a politician is rarely quiet."

"That's for sure," Benedict mumbled. When everyone looked his way, he explained, "My father has barely been at home since he agreed to step in as temporary leader of the House of Lords. There are so many new members joining Parliament that the existing party members have had to divvy them up in order to get them all settled in a timely fashion."

Rex noticed a cheeky smile spreading across Dora's face. "What are you plotting over there?"

"Don't mind me," she said, waving him off. "I was busy imagining how my mother must be keeping herself occupied."

"There's no need to imagine. She's forced me to squire her around town for visiting hours, suppers, and even a society ball." Benedict scowled at the memory. His confirmation only made Dora smile more widely.

Rex sympathised with the man's position. It was no accident

that the Duchess of Dorset dragged her eldest son from one society event to another. It would take all the Cavendish infamous steely determination to keep Benedict from finding himself standing at the altar before summer's end.

Harris took the reins of the conversation in hand before the siblings could resort to bickering. He consulted his notepad and made a few annotations. "I'll put the Murphys at the top of my list for now. Don't take that to mean that they are guilty, however. They have been forthcoming about their connection to the count, which is more than I can say for Lord Lambert. Despite what the man claims, there must be a reason the count wanted them to be here this weekend. If the Lamberts claim to have no knowledge, we will ask someone else."

"My grandmother?" Rex asked.

Harris nodded. "Yes, she is certainly a source which we'll consult. I'd also like to pose the question to Sir Elmer."

Dora stood from her seat on the sofa and walked around to stretch her legs. "While you're busy interrogating our guests, what would you like us to do?"

"Find something to keep everyone else occupied," Harris said. "The last thing we need is for everyone to sit around with too much time on their hands. They might do something rash and undermine our progress."

"We can hardly propose a round of party games," Dora countered. "But if the weather will hold, we could take everyone outdoors. Maybe even play croquet on the lawn. We'd be close enough for people to come and go as you need them, Harris."

A harsh knock on the door interrupted the discussion. The man Harris had introduced as Smith burst into the room.

"Boss, we've got a problem."

Harris leapt to his feet. Rex, Dora, and Benedict didn't want

Lynn Morrison

to be left behind. They were fast on Harris's heels while he dashed down the corridor to the front entrance.

Smith was a few steps ahead. He had the front door open by the time they caught up.

The first thing Rex noticed was the cloud of dust in the drive. It took a moment for him to realise that a car was speeding in the midst of it. A white Rolls-Royce, if he wasn't mistaken.

The driver of the car tooted the horn and waved his hand. He was completely oblivious to the person giving him chase. One of Harris's 'officers' pedalled madly on a bicycle, doing his best to stay in hot pursuit.

"Who is that?" Harris asked. He turned round and looked to Benedict. "Are we expecting any other surprise guests?"

Benedict was as mystified.

Rex, however, was not. He had ridden in that particular car too many times not to recognise both the model and the driver.

"Oh no," he groaned. "Oh, no no no..."

"My word! It's Lord Clark!" Dora gasped, clocking onto the man's identity at the same time.

"Should I send him away?" Smith asked.

"I daresay that will be impossible," Rex said, holding out a hand to stop the man from dashing off. "He obviously blew past the man at the gate. Now that he's seen us, there's no way he will depart without asking what is going on."

The car was already slowing as it made the turn in front of the house. Lord Clark Kenworthy, the eldest son of Earl Rivers, beamed from ear to ear beneath his moustache. He stepped on the brakes and the car slid to a stop. After switching it off, he climbed out.

"What ho, old chums!" he cried in delight. "It's jolly good to see your faces. Although you didn't have to rush out to meet me. Why, I'd almost think you were expecting me!"

By then, the officer at the gate had caught up on his bicycle.

The poor man's face was flushed, and he was clearly out of breath. Harris sent Smith over to update his colleague before the situation got any worse.

Although that was nigh impossible for Rex to imagine.

This was supposed to be a quiet weekend, with an easy-to-accomplish task of spying on a guest. Instead, Rex had a corpse, a murderer, a mishmash of guests, a pair of rival siblings, his grandmother, and now, London's most notorious prankster.

Rex's mettle flagged. He was only human, after all. His mouth opened and closed like a fish gasping in the air. Half composed sentences died on his lips.

Clark bounded across the drive to the foot of the front doorstep. His eyes twinkled with mirth as he bowed over Dora's outstretched hand and kissed her knuckles.

"Miss Laurent, you are as ravishing as ever. Please tell me you've grown bored with Rex and are ready to venture into new pastures."

"Good grief," Benedict grumbled loud enough for Rex to overhear.

Dora, ever the stalwart in the face of a challenge, fluttered her lashes at Clark's flowing compliments. "I'm afraid if that is the reason for your unexpected visit, you're in for a disappointment."

Clark straightened up and seemed none the worse for Dora's brush off. "You speak in absolutes when the weekend has barely begun. There's time yet for everything, I say!" He took a step back to survey the group. "Rex, Lord Benedict, and Harris? Has something happened to Percival? Why is Theodora's butler manning Percival's station?"

"That's the first odd thing he notices?" Benedict's rhetorical question hung in the air.

Rex had a hard time keeping a straight face. His life had devolved into a farce that was so outlandish it wasn't even fit for the stage. The only saving grace was that none of the other guests had been around to hear Clark's question.

He tossed an arm over Clark's shoulders and herded him into the house. "Let's get you something to wash the travel dust out of your mouth and I'll explain everything."

Or, almost everything...

Rex tossed a desperate glance over his shoulder. Dora, coming in behind him, exuded a calm he certainly didn't feel. Fortunately, she mouthed the one phrase capable of calming his nerves.

"We'll figure it out!"

Chapter 15
That time in Ireland

Dora breathed a sigh of relief when Rex accepted her statement at face value. Unfortunately, not everyone was as confident in her ability to think on her feet.

While Rex steered Clark toward the privacy of the library, Benedict latched onto Dora's arm.

"Get rid of him," he hissed at her.

Although that had been Dora's plan, hearing Benedict give her orders set her back teeth on edge. "Before finding out why he's here?"

Benedict's face flushed with anger. "First your butler, now that fool of a man. I'm calling Father again. You are in over your head."

Dora twisted her arm and flicked her wrist so that now she was the one holding Benedict in place. She sank her nails into the fabric of his sweater. "You want to call home, then fine. I won't stop you. In fact, I'll even request the number from the exchange. But the moment you do, you are out. Of this... of everything. Ask yourself this question: what's more important to you? Being *right* now or discovering how many times in the past you've been wrong. You cannot have it both ways."

Dora released her hold on Benedict as quickly as she'd taken it. She didn't bother waiting for an answer. Instead, she spun around and marched off.

With his hands balled into fists at his side, Benedict watched her walk away. Dora never had understood where to draw the line between game time and seriousness. She waltzed through life, blind to the repercussions of her decisions. Although reason told him to leave, he stuck around. Someone would have to save Dora from herself.

Harris waited in the door to the library. Rex and Clark stood further inside.

Clark was staring in confusion at the strange sight of two large travel trunks in the middle of the library floor. He leaned over to get a closer look at the contents of the one they'd left open.

Dora had to think fast. She hurried around the furniture and closed the top of the trunk. "It's a new parlour game," she explained. "You ask the staff to bring down a case and then we all try to guess to whom it belongs."

Clark's confusion lifted, but he wasn't completely satisfied with her explanation. "Don't take this the wrong way, but that doesn't sound at all fun. If you're going to paw through someone's underwear, I can think of much more entertaining ways to do so."

Dora had to bite her lip to keep from laughing. She held tight to her composure. "Yes, we arrived at the same conclusion. But it is of no matter, because now you're here. To what do we owe the honour of your unexpected presence?"

Clark chose the two-seater sofa and sprawled across it as though he didn't have a care in the world. He smiled at Dora and Rex and waved for them to sit down.

Benedict and Harris hung back. They remained close to the door, waiting to see how Dora and Rex were going to deal with the situation. Rex looked at his hapless friend and then over at Dora.

It wasn't Rex's fault he was so discombobulated. None of his training exercises had prepared him for having an innocent bystander wander into the middle of a mission.

That was something Dora would have to rectify, but first, she needed to deal with Clark.

"You mentioned something about a drink?" Clark reminded Rex. He glanced over his shoulder at Harris, waiting for the butler to leap into action.

"Of course, my lord," Harris said in an apologetic tone. He hurried over to the bar cart. Dora watched while he poured a splash of whiskey and two cubes of ice into a crystal glass, and topped it with water before delivering it to Clark.

Clark took a great gulp and then smacked his lips in satisfaction. "Travelling always makes me work up a great thirst. Now, where were we?"

"You're just about to tell us why you were here," Dora said. "And don't tell me you were in the neighbourhood. We're miles from anyone."

"Ahh, but that isn't strictly true," Clark countered. "Blenheim isn't more than an hour's drive away. I was there for a hunting party, under strict orders from my father," he added. "Dreary bunch of old men. I claimed to have a caught a chill so I could avoid another day of trooping through the woods. When they left, I leapt into my car and here I am!"

"And here you are!" Dora echoed. "While it's always lovely to see you, I'm afraid you've come at a bad time."

"How so?" Clark asked. "Does it have anything to do with the man at the front gate? I thought he was being friendly when he waved, but then he chased me on the bicycle."

And yet, Clark had blithely carried on up the drive. Clark's cluelessness had worked to their advantage when he'd stumbled across Dora and Rex, hiding in Westminster. But Dora had used the 'game' excuse far too many times with him.

They needed Clark gone, as quickly as possible, and certainly before any of their other guests came down to see who had arrived. Dora couldn't afford to waste time tap dancing around the truth.

He said he'd come to escape from a dreary weekend. Therefore, her best course of action was to convince him he'd gone from the proverbial boiling pot into the flames.

She sighed heavily and allowed her mouth to droop into a frown. "I'm terribly sorry, darling, but I fear we've little entertainment to offer. You see, we've got a house full of guests who are all duds. You'd be better off driving to Oxford and hitting up a friend there."

Clark glanced at Rex. Rex gave a suitably dour expression in reply. Even Benedict played along.

They were so close...

Clark did not take the bait. He sat up straight so quickly his drink threatened to slosh over the side of his glass. "Look at you all! So downcast! This is a travesty of the first order. What kind of friend would I be to leave you in such dire straights?"

"But you must," Rex blurted. "Grandmama is here as well. They're her guests. She won't be happy if we do our usual of running amuck. I'm afraid there's nothing to it. We'll survive, and there's no reason for you to suffer with us. Harris, be a good man and ask my driver to top up Lord Clark's petrol."

Clark, however, was not moving. The more they insisted he go, the further he entrenched himself on that sofa. He crossed his arms and leaned back. "Who are these guests?"

"No one you'd like," Rex answered. "Boring people."

"So boring you have a guard at the gate? What are you all up to here?"

Rex looked at Dora. Dora wanted to pass the responsibility

along the line, but it stopped with her. Where to start? The answer was obvious. "Lord and Lady Lambert."

Clark pulled a face. "Egads! He isn't too terrible, but the wife is beastly."

"Yes, exactly," Dora said. "And you can imagine how she's reacted to my presence."

"Staring down her nose at you, as though you are lower than the dust on her shoes?"

"Got it in one." Dora reassured Clark that she wasn't taking it personally. "As Rex said, his grandmother is here. I'm taking a certain delight in watching her take Lady Lambert to task."

Clark seemed mollified by Dora's answer. A spark of hope flared in her breast. Despite the guard at the gate, the presence of her butler, and the trunks in the library, somehow they were going to get rid of Clark before he unravelled their crazed plan to solve the count's murder.

"Who else?"

Dora's attention snapped back to the room. "What?"

"Who else is here?" Clark asked. "If it were only Lord and Lady Lambert, I can't imagine the dowager would expect you two to stay. So, there must be someone else on the guest list."

"Err, yes..." Dora reached for the next pair of names that came to mind. "A Mr and Mrs Murphy. We'd never met them before. Isn't that right, Rex?"

Rex nodded at her command. "They aren't exactly of our class, if you catch my drift. Nice enough, but not ones likely to capture your interest."

"Patrick and Gladys Murphy?" Clark asked.

Dora's stomach turned over.

"Of course I've met them," Clark insisted. "He's a rising star among the new MPs."

Movement across the room caught Dora's attention. It was Benedict. He had one hand on his head and appeared to be tugging on his hair. Half of Dora wanted to laugh. The other half agreed with him.

Unfortunately, Clark tracked the direction of her gaze. Benedict smoothly segued his hair-pulling into a gentle glide across his head, looking to all the world as though he'd been smoothing his hair into place.

"Is that why you're in residence, Lord Benedict? Has the duke sent you as his emissary to woo Mr Murphy into accepting a leadership position?"

"Something of that nature," Benedict muttered, demurring to reveal further detail.

"Well then, who else is there? Come now, you've given me the worst of the lot, I'm sure. Might as well work fast and rip the rest of the bandage off."

Benedict pressed his lips together. Rex shifted uncomfortably in his chair. Harris kept his expression perfectly blank, as befitting of a butler.

Dora was fast concluding that carrying Clark out to his car and driving him away wasn't such a bad idea after all. The man refused to take a hint.

Clark took another sip of his drink and then stared into the contents of the glass. "Wait, let me think. Shall we make this into a guessing game?"

Dora's plastic smile gave him all the encouragement he needed.

"The Lamberts and the Murphys, you've said. And then there's the guard at the gate. Who would warrant help fending off the attention of followers?" He mulled for much less time than Dora expected before blurting out an answer. "By Jove! It must be Count Vasile! Is Sir Elmer here as well? Last I saw them together, they had a veritable herd of women chasing after them. You must know him, Theodora. He's part of your international set."

The occupants of the room were so stunned that they momentarily forgot their plan to get rid of Clark. Their varying expressions of shock and awe caused Clark to burst into uproarious laughter.

"I've got it, haven't I? I'd claim prescience, but I owe it all to my last trip to Ireland. I saw the Lamberts, met the Murphys, and so it was only natural for my mind to wander further along the same path. Well, that's brilliant! Are you keeping the count's visit a secret? Worried the local papers will reveal the truth? My lips are sealed." To emphasise his point, Clark mimed pressing his lips together and sealing them shut.

Benedict recovered fastest. "Yes, old chap, you have it. And now you see why you must go. You'll throw the numbers off, and that always annoys women like the dowager."

Clark finally set his glass on the nearby side table and made a move to stand. "It won't do to have the dowager duchess be cross with me. But before I go, I'd love to pass my regards along to the count and Sir Elmer. We had a grand old time exploring Ireland's water holes. Harris, be a good man and send a footman to fetch them."

Harris inclined his head and said, "I will check whether either of the men is available."

"Wait," Dora called, bringing Harris to an abrupt halt. She turned back to Clark. "This trip you took to Ireland. Was it a few months ago?"

Clark confirmed the dates. "It was prior to the mess in the Chanak. Ahh, times were simpler then, weren't they?"

Dora ignored his question. She was too busy reassessing their entire investigation plan. Until then, Dora and her companions had been on the back foot. They knew little of the count's connections with the guests. They hadn't even seen the group interact. But Clark was different.

"You were there? With all the people I've mentioned?" she asked, seeking confirmation.

Clark looked askance at Dora. "That is what I said. Why are you staring at me? Do I have dirt on my face?"

His face was clear, but dirt was indeed what was on Dora's mind. She and the others needed to ferret out the insider gossip about Count Vasile's interactions with the others. She'd thought to lean upon the dowager's deep well of information, but Clark was even better. He had first-hand knowledge, and could act as a litmus test for what they learned while questioning the guests.

Had Lord and Lady Lambert truly never met the count?

Were Mr and Mrs Murphy only acquaintances?

Was there something else to learn about Sir Elmer's seemingly solid friendship?

She shot a glance at Harris. He tilted his head forward for a split second and then blinked twice, using their prearranged signal to show his approval.

That settled, she turned to Rex. Their partnership, for lack of a better term, was much newer. Dora wasn't sure he'd be able to parse the meaning of her raised eyebrows.

Whether he truly understood was irrelevant. He held her gaze, searching her face, and then flashed a hint of a smile. He was game for whatever she did next.

"Clark, take a seat," she said. "We've not been entirely truthful with you."

Benedict, still standing behind Clark, raised his hands into the air and waved them feverishly.

Dora ignored his attempts to stop her.

"We're in dire straits, Clark. More desperate than we've ever been before. Will you help us?"

Benedict choked back a growl, but his frantic slashes through the air conveyed his opinion.

Benedict, however, didn't know Clark the way Dora did.

Benedict didn't know anyone there the way Dora did. He was blind to the hidden skill sets which made every member of her team so useful.

Inga had been right. Dora had to tell him everything, starting with the full truth about her journey from Dorothy Cavendish to Theodora Laurent.

But first, she had to bring Clark into the fold. She and Rex had leaned upon their friend twice now. He'd leapt to their aid when they sought Freddie's killer. He'd come through with information at a critical moment in their last case. Who's to say he wouldn't do the same thing again?

Clark's attention never shifted from Dora's face. He sat down, but this time remained sitting fully upright. All hints of insouciance disappeared from his expression. He was as deadly serious as she was.

"Theodora, you have only to ask. I'll always come through when you and Rex need a friend."

Chapter 16
News from the rumour mill

B enedict was fit to be tied, but Rex didn't question Dora's judgement. If she thought telling Clark some version of the truth was the right thing to do, then it was. Not for a second did he expect her to come clean over all of it. She trusted Clark to be an ally, but her true purpose for being in England was on a need to know basis.

Clark didn't need that information.

Rex, however, had to get Benedict out of the room before he said something to give away his connection to Dora. No upper class man would descend into an argument with a woman in front of a group. But he'd seen enough of Dora and Benedict's interactions to admit that was a distinct possibility. With Dora sent off to school at a young age, their sibling relationship remained frozen in their childhood years. They hadn't learned how to interact as adults.

"Benedict," Rex said, to get the man's attention. "Would you mind checking whether my grandmother will join us?"

Benedict opened his mouth to argue, but shut it when he saw Rex's stony gaze. The request was an excuse to get him out of the room. He huffed, but left it at that. "I was planning to get a book from my room, anyway. I can knock on her door while I pass."

Rex hadn't meant to shove Benedict completely aside. He clarified, "Fetch whatever you need, but please do come back with her. We'll need everyone's guidance."

Somewhat mollified, Benedict left.

When the door closed behind him, Rex invited Harris to take a seat and then he turned the floor over to Dora.

"There's no way to start other than to blurt it out," she said. "Count Vasile is dead and our guests have accused Rex of murdering him."

Clark stared slack-jawed at Dora and then burst out laughing. "Oh, darling Theodora! For a moment, I almost believed you. That was a terrible joke to play on me."

"I'm not joking."

"She's really not," Harris added. It was his words, more than anything else, that got through to Clark.

Clark wiped the grin from his face. "My word! I apologise for making light. But, it is so farfetched, you can hardly blame me!"

Dora rushed to smooth his feathers. "I assure you, we took no offence. Honestly, I wish this were all some kind of joke, rather than a waking nightmare. Now that we've told you the worst, we'll start from the beginning."

Rex had a front-row seat as Dora wove a tale of truths and half-truths at the start, and ending with blatant lies. Yes, Count Vasile was an old friend of Dora, whom they'd invited to a weekend in the countryside. She told Clark they'd allowed Vasile to build the guest list, but left off the reasons. As for the dowager duchess and Lord Benedict, they'd been last-minute additions, as unexpected as Clark himself.

"And you found him dead?" Clark asked Rex after Dora got

to that point in the story. "That must have been terrible for you."

His friend's concern touched Rex's heart. "It is most definitely not a practice I care to repeat. I called for Dora, so I could tell her in private. Then the two of us descended to the drawing room where everyone had gathered for drinks."

"Rex barely had time to get the words out before the accusations started flying. They accused me of having a longstanding relationship with the count and said Rex had acted out of jealousy."

"But that's absurd!" Clark was having none of it. "I've spent more time with you two than most, and there is no doubt in mind as to the threads of love that bind you together. I'll tell them all. They'll have to see reason."

Dora's gut lurched at Clark's poignant description of her connection to Rex. It was one more reminder of how far over the line she'd allowed things to go. Even if nothing had happened between the two of them, their lingering glances and touches gave the appearance they were deeply in love.

Now, however, wasn't the time to correct Clark's misunderstanding.

Dora laid her hands over her chest and sighed heavily. "Oh Clark, I wish it were that simple. If you'd been here last night, maybe that would have been enough. But the thought took hold like a spreading mania. You know how these small-town constables can be. You think they have much experience dealing with crimes within the upper crust? They'd have latched onto Rex being a murderer without a moment of hesitation. I couldn't let that happen, so I asked Harris for help."

"Harris?" Clark turned to the man in question.

"I'm a retired detective. I told Dora we had to buy ourselves a few days — three tops — to identify the killer before bringing in any outsiders. As you rightly pointed out, I'm not part of the dowager's household. Since I'm a stranger to the guests, I dragged out my old suit and showed up in the role of local police."

Clark's astonishment shifted to admiration. "That was a perilous move, for all of you, but especially Harris. What if you get caught?"

"We won't," Dora said, cutting in. "This is why we encouraged you to leave when you first came in. But as we spoke, I realised your arrival was a blessing in disguise. You've met all the players in this game. Will you help us figure out who is the killer?"

"It isn't without risks, as you rightly pointed out, but we've done everything we can to mitigate them." Harris stood again and smoothed his suit. He held still while Clark studied him. "If we hadn't met before, would you guess my real identity?"

"No. Not at all." Clark twisted his moustache. "I said before I would help, and my answer hasn't changed. Tell me what I can do."

"You can help us fill in the gaps of our knowledge about our guests," Rex said. A knock on the door prevented him from speaking further. "Come in."

As expected, it was his grandmother, accompanied by Benedict. While Clark paid his respects to the dowager duchess, Rex rang for a fresh pot of tea.

After Percival delivered the steaming teapot, cups, and saucers, Harris gave him an additional request.

"Would you alert the other guests that I'm here, and will call for them one-by-one to meet me in the drawing room? They've likely heard the flurry of activity downstairs and will wonder what is going on."

Percival inclined his head and left to follow the orders.

Dora offered to play mother while the men rearranged the seats to accommodate their now larger group. They stacked the trunks against the far wall and pulled up two extra chairs. They ended up with an intimate circle, where they could all speak as equals. Dora and the dowager took the two-seater sofa, while the men took the chairs. Rex and Harris sat on Dora's right, while Benedict and Clark completed the circle by sitting to the dowager's left.

Rex's grandmother thanked Dora for the cup of tea. She added two sugars and gave it a quick stir. "As the most senior member of this group, it falls to me to set the tenor of our conversations. Rex's freedom, and perhaps even his life, is on the line. Therefore, I suggest we set aside our titles and societal obligations and speak frankly with one another. Does anyone wish to disagree?"

Benedict opened his mouth, but one look at Dora's stony glare had him shutting it again. All around them, the other members of the inner circle held their tongues.

"Excellent. We have one more member, Miss Inga Kay, Dora's companion. She is momentarily absent, having dashed off to Ducklington village on an errand. Other than us, everyone else is to be treated with a modicum of suspicion."

"Even the servants?" Clark asked.

The dowager pursed her lips. "I'm confident my household is safe, but we have the Lambert's valet and lady's maid to consider. The fewer people who know the full truth of what we are about, the better."

"I agree," Dora said. "For the benefit of those who haven't been part of all our conversations, I will provide a brief recount of what we've learned so far. Sir Elmer is Vasile's dear friend, of some long standing. Mr and Mrs Murphy briefly met Vasile at an event, but claimed not to be close with him. Last but not least, Lord and Lady Lambert say the man was a stranger to them. Nonetheless, each of our guests was hand-picked by the count."

Dora motioned to the man sitting beside the dowager. "Clark's timely arrival has brought us further information. He has placed all our guests in Ireland during the same time frame. Edith, what can you add to our knowledge?"

Rex fixed his gaze on his grandmother. She sipped her tea while appearing to be in deep thought. Having cloistered herself away with Inga for most of the morning, she hadn't heard about Lord Lambert's claim. As expected, she addressed that first.

"I've known Lillian Lambert since before her debut. The woman is quick to flaunt her associations with those above her in the pecking order. Although Count Vasile wasn't British, his title was cachet enough to attract her attention. If Lord Lambert said they never met the man, I'm inclined to believe him."

"But I saw the Lamberts in Ireland when I travelled over to a wedding."

"They were there, and probably should have met the count, but they didn't, and I know why."

With that phrase, the dowager had everyone's attention.

"As Clark said, three months ago, the Earl of Egmont hosted a gathering at his family estate in Ireland on the occasion of his youngest daughter's wedding. Unlike Clark, the timing wasn't right for me to go, so I sent my apologies. I did, however, make a note of which of my circle of friends made the trip. When they returned, I invited them for tea so I could learn the gossip."

"And that is why we so value your presence, Edith," Dora said while patting Edith's hand.

"Count Vasile cut a dashing figure and left many a tongue wagging. That alone was reason enough for me to choose to join you this weekend. Unfortunately, much like the case of the Lamberts, an introduction to Count Vasile was not to be."

"What happened with the Lamberts?" Dora asked.

"Lord and Lady Lambert never made it to the wedding. They cut their trip short after the Lambert family pearls disappeared from their stateroom in their hotel in Dublin. Lillian was so distraught over the theft that she demanded to return home."

"Ahh, yes, that rings a bell." Clark scratched his chin. "I spotted the Lamberts in the hotel dining room one evening. Lady Lambert wore her usual sneer of disgust. It was enough to put me off my food. I went elsewhere and ended up running into Sir Elmer and Count Vasile. When the Lamberts didn't turn up at the wedding, I remember hearing people gossiping about a kerfuffle, but I didn't pay attention to the details. It's never in your best interest to question why the stars align in your favour. Avoiding Lady Lambert was enough for me."

"Unfortunately, your luck has run out, dear boy. The size of our intimate weekend party prevents any of us from avoiding Lady Lambert and her spiteful remarks. I'll do my best to keep her in hand, but I make no promises. Last night, she lashed out at me — performing a feat I'd have thought beyond her capabilities. Murder seems to have loosened her tongue from what little restraint society induced her to exercise."

There was no point in complaining. Rex recalled what his grandmama had said the last time he'd asked permission to avoid spending time with a noxious guest. "*Bono malum superate*," she'd said, letting the Latin phrase roll off her tongue. Unacceptable behaviour only improved when good people were there to keep the miscreants in check.

Rex was certain neither titles nor fortunes would sway Lady Lambert from making everyone in Ducklington Manor miserable.

Chapter 17
Dora goes undercover

Dora had already resigned herself to a weekend of cutting remarks and snotty innuendos, so the dowager's warning raised no additional concerns. Instead, Dora fit the news of a potential Irish connection into the bigger picture.

The waxing and waning battles for control over Ireland were exactly the type of scenario Count Vasile preferred, at least, as far as Dora knew. While the local inhabitants paid the highest price during such conflicts, men like Vasile grew rich, funnelling money and weapons to either side.

But things in Ireland were finally calming. The last of the British troops in the Irish Free State were due to leave before the end of the year. Why would Count Vasile be involved so late in the game?

Dora didn't like the direction of her thoughts. The Irish peace, such as it was, could be best described as fragile. Had Vasile wanted to undermine the stability of the nascent state? If so, why? Who would gain from such an outcome?

More importantly, which of their house guests was most likely to be involved? The Murphys rose to the top of the list, but perhaps that had been Vasile's goal all along. With them in plain sight, who would think to watch the others?

Dora wanted to know more about this supposed theft and the Lambert's subsequent hasty departure from Dublin. She had the view from above. Now she needed the one from below... below stairs, that is.

It was time to go undercover.

Dora placed her cup and saucer on the table and asked to be excused. "Harris will need to move into the drawing room soon. I'll go speak with the housekeeper about arranging a lunch buffet on the terrace so we can draw everyone outside."

She studiously avoided catching Rex's eye as she made her departure. Once she was safe in the corridor, she took a moment to lean against the wall and calm her thoughts. Although Clark's arrival brought much needed information, it had also introduced a new wrinkle to her plans to keep Rex at arm's length. She couldn't afford for anyone to suspect trouble in their lover's paradise.

She'd taken great care to keep her distance from him in the library, for once not snuggling into his side on the sofa. Sleuthing might buy her more time on her own, but the next time they were around the larger group, she'd have to keep up the romantic facade.

What had seemed like the easiest part of her weekend now sat atop the list of problems.

The scrape of a nearby door opening jerked Dora from her reverie. Fortunately, it was one of her twin footmen. She had to wait for him to get close enough to see clearly to work out which one.

"Ah Basel, I'm so glad it's you, as I need some help. Can you tell the housekeeper we'll dine outside? Help her with whatever she needs. On your way to doing that, could you find your sister and ask her to meet me in my room?"

"Of course, Miss Laurent," he answered. "Cynthia first and then lunch arrangements."

Dora hurried up the stairs and into her bedroom. She made straight for her dressing room, where she set to work getting out of her own clothing.

"You sent for me, Miss?" Cynthia asked as she came through the door.

Dora stuck her head through the doorway and motioned for the maid to come closer. "I need a uniform and my wig. Use the secret passageway. I'll wait here."

Cynthia didn't need to be asked twice. They'd prepared in advance for this contingency. Cynthia had a battered suitcase stored under her bed, with Dora's wigs, prosthetics, and stage make-up stored inside. By the time she returned, Dora had twisted and pinned her strawberry blonde locks so they'd fit under the wig.

While Dora got dressed, she explained the plan. "I need to speak with the Lambert's lady's maid. Any suggestions on how we can arrange that?"

"She asked me this morning if I knew of a sunny spot where she could do some sewing. If you don't mind using a needle and thread, that would be my recommendation."

Dora didn't mind in the least. "We can use the old nursery rooms upstairs. Give me something small to work on so I can have an excuse to leave once I finish."

"I'll do you one better. Miss Dixon asked if I could repair the hem on her skirt. You can claim to be extra help come over from the village."

Dora reached over and gave Cynthia a squeeze. The young maid was so caught off guard, she squeaked.

"I'm so glad your brothers told me about you. Your myriad of talents was wasted on a life of crime."

Cynthia blushed. "I always feared going straight would

leave me in the doldrums, but criminal life didn't require half as much misbehaviour from me as you do." She gave Dora's wig a few strokes with the brush and then helped her pin her cap in place. The addition of carefully applied stage make-up and a pair of glasses completed the disguise. "Good enough. Go upstairs first and arrange the chairs so you're somewhat in the shadows."

Dora used the secret passage to slip away unseen. She followed it to an opening into the main corridor, and from there, crossed over to the servant's staircase. The nursery sat in the southeast corner of the house. Most of the furniture hid under the white sheets protecting them from dust, but there were a few simple wooden chairs left free. Dora shifted them into place in front of the largest window and barely had time to take her seat before Cynthia returned.

The woman accompanying her appeared to be in her middle years. Her thick black hair showed traces of silver and crow's feet marked the outside corners of her eyes. She was otherwise of average height and weight. Dressed in a navy dress with a white apron, she carried herself with the posture of a woman resigned to remaining in the background.

Cynthia took the middle seat for herself and waved for the Lambert's maid to join them. "This is Mary. She's Lady Lambert's lady's maid. Mary, meet Polly."

Dora nodded her head in welcome, taking care to keep her face out of the direct sunlight.

Cynthia went straight to work. She opened her bag of sewing and removed a pale blue dress. "Here you are, Polly. I was telling Mary on the way up how grateful I am for you lending a hand this weekend. We're short two lady's maids and the result is I've been run off my feet. I never thought I'd be happy to sit down with a needle and thread, but at least it's time to catch my breath."

"I wondered how you were getting on," Mary replied. "Her ladyship spent all of her toilette complaining about the lack of quality guests. She didn't settle down until I told her I'd spotted Lady Rockingham arrive."

Dora took care to modulate her voice and tweak her accent until she sounded nothing like herself. "I don't know how you can find the courage to speak in front of a real Lady. I'd be scared stiff if the dowager duchess even so much as glanced my way."

Mary gave her a friendly smile. "I remember feeling the same way when I started. I was a housemaid first, but her ladyship requested I join her when she left to get married. She wanted a familiar face in her new household, I guess. Since everyone else was a veritable stranger, her ladyship began confiding in me."

"Wow!" Dora gasped, looking suitably impressed. She flicked her needle through the hem, whipping it into place. It was just one skill she'd picked up while volunteering on the front line. At least now, she was sewing fabric instead of wounds. But now wasn't the time for those thoughts.

She turned her mind back to the task at hand — gathering information about the Lamberts. She nudged the conversation in the right direction. "And now you get to travel everywhere she goes. I've never made farther away than Oxford. I bet you've seen more of the world."

Mary grimaced. "Lord and Lady Lambert prefer to remain within the confines of the British shores, if at all possible. French food gives Lord Lambert indigestion. Egypt and India are far too hot for Lady Lambert's tastes."

"So you've been nowhere at all?" Dora gasped, looking suitably disappointed.

Mary snipped the ends of her thread to free her needle for her next project. "I made the mistake of getting my hopes up earlier this year when her ladyship announced we were going to Ireland. Of course, that trip ended so badly, now I fear we'll never go anywhere again. Other than houses like this," she hastened to add.

"Ducklington Manor is grand," Cynthia said, joining into the conversation. "But we're barely far enough away from London to get a breath of fresh air. Now, you can't leave us with that tidbit of information. Where in Ireland did you go and what happened?"

Dora worried that Cynthia's blunt question would cause Mary to clam up, but she never should have doubted her trusted maid.

Mary lowered her sewing into her lap and checked the room to make sure no one was nearby. Never mind that they were in an empty wing of the house. Then she leaned forward and spoke in a low voice. "Normally I wouldn't speak any ill about my mistress, but given she's ranted and raved about this to everyone who came within ten feet of her, I'll make an exception. We went to Dublin where she was robbed."

"No!" Dora and Cynthia gasped in perfect unison.

Mary's eyes opened wide as she nodded her head. "The famed family pearls, if you can believe it."

"But where? In a house like this one?" Cynthia asked.

"Oh no, such a thing would never happen in a place like this..." Mary's voice trailed off, and they all frowned. Something much worse had happened in Ducklington Manor, not that any of them wanted to venture toward that topic.

Dora moved fast to intercede. "Where were you, then?"

Mary stuck her needle into the bundle of fabric so she could focus her full attention on her willing audience. "We had a rough crossing, you see. Instead of taking a car straight to the big house where the wedding was to be held, Lady Lambert demanded we stay put in Dublin until her stomach calmed. His lordship's valet had to hustle around town searching for last-minute accommodation. We ended up in a grand hotel, far nicer than anything his lordship would have chosen on his own. Well, as you can imagine, Lady Lambert was content to sit tight for several days in such lavish surroundings."

"Oh! I bet it was like something you'd see in the picture shows!" Cynthia cooed.

Dora shifted her gaze to her maid and saw a flash of wistful longing cross the woman's face. Unlike Dora, Cynthia wasn't feigning envy. The young woman likely had never been further away than the seaside. When this was said and done, Dora would find a way to change that.

"Even though I was a servant, the hotel still treated me like a guest. A lower-class guest, but if I rang for tea and biscuits, they brought it up, all the same." Mary stared off into the distance, her mind back in Dublin. "When it came time for my half-day off, Lady Lambert gave me permission to walk around town, provided I stay with his lordship's valet. That's how the hotel room ended up empty for a few hours. It wasn't until her ladyship dressed for dinner, that we discovered the theft. The pearls were nowhere to be found."

Mary's eyes filled with tears, but she blinked them away.

Cynthia reached out a hand. "Did you get blamed? At first, I mean?"

Mary nodded. "But I'd been with Bert all day, along with a guide from the hotel. They never let me out of their sight. Still, the hotel security searched all our bags. It was no use. The necklace was gone. Lady Lambert bawled her eyes out. Said she couldn't remain in Ireland for another minute. This was what happened when upstanding English gentlemen and ladies ventured too far from their homes."

Dora let Cynthia make the appropriate noises in response.

There was something Mary had said earlier, a point that had caught Dora's attention.

She remembered. "Mary, why'd you say that the hotel was nicer than Lord Lambert would have chosen? Surely people like them only stay in the nicest places wherever they go."

For the first time, Mary slammed her mouth shut and refused to breathe a word. Dora's mind raced through the implications. She'd had plenty of experience with families who worked hard at keeping up appearances. She just hadn't expected Lord and Lady Lambert to be in that position.

"Land rich, are they?" she asked. "I read about those kinds of families in those old books by Miss Austen. If you ask me, it's far better to know your place in the world and be happy with it than to have to live up to aspirations you can't afford."

Mary leaned close for the last time and spoke in a voice barely louder than a whisper. "I'll call you a liar if you repeat this, but part of me wondered whether the necklace was really stolen." She wiggled her eyebrows.

"Lady Lambert?" Cynthia whispered.

"No, not her. She's no actress, that one. Every thought that crosses her mind plays out across her face. But his lordship? He'd do anything to avoid her ire..."

"Anything?" Dora asked, looking properly scandalised.

Mary gave a single nod. "Anything."

Chapter 18
A ghastly confession

R ex crept from his bedroom to Dora's, using the hidden passageway. He didn't expect to find her inside, and was therefore not disappointed when he found the room empty.

When she'd excused herself from the group claiming the need to organise the luncheon, he'd been all but certain that she had something else planned. Dora rarely involved herself in household matters, and was even less likely given Rex's grandmother's presence.

He recognised the maroon sweater draped across the back of her dressing table chair as the one she'd had on earlier in the day. Not only away, but also in costume? Rex decided he'd stay put until she returned. He doubted it would be too long, given she had offered no excuse for an extended absence.

In the meantime, he opened the book he'd taken from the library shelf. All the talk of Ireland had reminded him of a new book he'd spotted shortly after their arrival at Ducklington. With the title of *Ulysses* printed on the spine, Rex had skipped the thick volume, assuming it to be a mythology reference. But Clark's mention of Dublin reminded Rex that he'd seen parts of the story serialised in back copies of America's *The Little Review*. He needed to brush up on his understanding of twentieth century Ireland, and one could do worse than consulting James Joyce.

He made only a little headway before a brunette housemaid entered the room. He tempered his initial urge to hide, recognising the familiar shade of Dora's favourite wig under the white maid's cap.

She balked at the sight of him sitting in her wingback chair. "Did anyone see you come in?"

"Of course not," he replied. "I used the passageway. Everything okay?"

"What? Oh, yes. Yes, all is fine. You caught me off guard, is all. I popped upstairs with Cynthia, where we had a natter with the Lambert's lady's maid."

"Well done! Did you learn anything useful?" Rex patted the arm of his chair, hinting she should sit down. Usually, that was one of Dora's favourite spots. Today, however, she shuffled awkwardly before choosing to lean against the wall.

"The maid confirmed the rumour. Lord and Lady Lambert went to Ireland for the wedding, but detoured to Dublin for a brief stay to recover from seasickness. Shortly after their arrival, the thief struck. Lady Lambert had a conniption, and they returned to England without attending the party."

"Anything about Count Vasile in all of that?"

Dora froze. "Err, I didn't ask her. That is, I couldn't ask her that. I was supposed to be from the village. There's no reason for an outsider to make a connection between Ireland, the Lamberts, and the count."

Dora's explanation made perfect sense, but her body language was all wrong. After the hours of work she'd made Rex put into interpreting those cues, Rex's mind immediately clocked onto the discrepancy.

Why was she standing so far away from him? And fidgeting? He'd never seen Dora fidget in his life. Theodora Laurent would never do something so pedestrian.

"You're sure you're okay?" Rex asked again. "Is it Benedict? Clark's sudden arrival? You seem off-kilter."

He barely got the words out of his mouth before Dora dropped her hands to her sides and straightened her posture. Seconds later, she was back to her normal, confident self.

"It's Benedict. I shouldn't let him get to me, but he can be a bit much. Especially when his doubts and digs come on top of everything else. Not to worry, though. I'll shake it off and be right as rain by luncheon."

Something was off with Dora's explanation. It rang true, but also hollow. Still, she'd tell him if he'd done something. It was best for them both if he stopped prying.

"I wouldn't expect Benedict to change his behaviour that quickly. As soon as you left the room, he suggested again that we phone the police."

Dora jerked. "In front of Clark?"

"Yes, and let me tell you, Grandmama was not pleased with him. She levelled one of her death glares on him and he wisely silenced himself before she did it for him."

Dora chuckled. "I'd have paid good money to see that. Still, we can't rely on her to always be there. I am loath to say it, but we've still no choice but to bring Benedict closer to the investigation, despite how much I'd rather push him away."

Rex's stomach burned at that thought. However, Dora was probably right. She had an excellent track record of reading people. Besides, they didn't have another option. Benedict wasn't going anywhere.

Dora tapped her chin. "I learned one other thing during my chat. The Lamberts are struggling to keep up appearances. Their maid insinuated that the so-called theft might have been cover for them selling the jewellery. Lord Lambert, that is. She said he'd do anything to make his wife happy."

Rex fit that information into what they'd learned so far. He spotted a possible connection. Although tenuous, it warranted asking. "Might Lord Lambert have given the necklace to Count Vasile? Perhaps as payment for an investment? If that were the case, and the investment failed to pay off, I could envision Lord Lambert being angry enough to do something. Killing Count Vasile, I'm not sure."

"Lady Lambert would do it." Dora's expression was grim. "The woman is one of the most self-entitled people I've ever met, and that's saying something. If she found out Count Vasile conned her husband out of their meagre funds, she'd strike out."

Rex didn't disagree. However, he hadn't a clue what to do next. "Should we talk to Grandmama? Get the two of them together and see if we can force a confession?"

"No. I have something different in mind. You've obviously found some kind of rapport with Lord Lambert. Why don't you and Benedict corner him and see if you can extract a confession? If his wife is unaware of what he did, he won't say anything with her around. But a conversation strictly between men of his social class... that might do the trick."

"It might," Rex agreed, although privately he questioned the wisdom of bringing Benedict along with him. Nothing for it but to go on.

"I spotted Lord Lambert in the games room. If I hurry, Benedict and I can catch him there." Rex held his book up. "I'll return this to my room on the way. Shall we meet you for lunch on the terrace when we're done? Theodora, that is. Not housemaid Dora."

Rex's joke coaxed a smile from Dora, just as he'd intended. "Believe it or not, I'm actually looking forward to a rousing round of croquet on the lawn. Every time I swing my mallet, I'll imagine I'm knocking it against my brother's head."

Rex saw his way out through the hidden doorway and in two shakes of a lamb's tail, he was back in the main corridor after a brief detour to his room. Benedict occupied the Salix bedroom, which was around the corner from Rex's room. He answered at the first knock.

"Did you need something, Lord Rex?"

"Might you want to accompany me to the games room for a round of billiards?" Rex asked. However, rather than moving aside so Benedict could leave the room, he indicated Benedict should invite him inside.

Benedict stepped back and motioned for Rex to come in. After securely fastening the door, Benedict looked to Rex for an explanation.

"We believe there may be more to the story of the stolen Lambert necklace. I intend to question him, and would appreciate your help."

Instead of agreeing, Benedict replied with a slew of questions. "Who is this we? And where did you get new information? We only left the library a quarter of an hour ago."

Rex answered with as little detail as possible. "From the Lambert's lady's maid. She was with them on the trip to Ireland."

Benedict seemed willing to accept that explanation, but he still refused to move. "Who questioned her? Was it Harris? I thought he was speaking with the Murphys."

"Does it matter?" Rex wanted to pull his hair out, but he reined in his temper. "Dora spoke to the maid while wearing a disguise. You'd be amazed how effective she is at role playing the lower classes."

"Not that again!" Benedict rolled his eyes toward the

heavens. "She and Will followed the housemaids and footman around, mimicking their every word. I can see she still hasn't outgrown her childhood entertainment."

Rex didn't bother correcting Benedict. Nothing any of them said was getting through. He'd be better off arguing with the willow tree beside the lake than attempting to convince Benedict to keep an open mind. At some point, the pile of evidence pointing towards Dora's competence would grow too large for the man to ignore.

"We'll get more out of Lambert if we take a sideways approach to the matter. Follow my lead."

Rex left the room with Benedict close behind, doing as he was told. They used the main staircase to descend to the public rooms and followed the marble floor to the entrance to the games room.

The door was half open, providing a partial view inside. Rex spotted Lord Lambert trying his hand at darts.

"Ahh, Lambert, just the man I wanted to see," he said, announcing their arrival in a booming voice.

Lord Lambert threw the dart in his hand before turning to face them. Rex bit back a grimace when the pointed tip drove into the silk wallpaper rather than the felt-covered board. If they got stuck inside, he'd suggest Dora offer the man lessons.

"I don't like to talk business on the weekend, but the circumstances are hardly typical. Lord Benedict and I got into a discussion of racing and he alerted me to a rare opportunity to acquire a pair of fillies from his stable. I only have space for one, but thought you might want the other." Rex turned to Benedict and gave him a meaningful look.

"Err, yes," Benedict said, slowly rising to the challenge. "My trainers have assured me they'll fetch top value at auction, but I'd be willing to forego the extra effort. What say you?"

Lord Lambert marched over to the wall to retrieve his dart, keeping his face turned away from the men. "That's a generous opportunity, but I'll have to pass. My interest in racing is waning."

"Really?" Rex professed his surprise. "But this morning, I noticed you turning straight to the racing page in the papers when I got up to leave."

Lord Lambert stiffened. "Old habit," he said. "I've sold off my stable, if you must know the truth."

Rex and Benedict exchanged glances. The Lambert stables were renowned, and had been so for several generations. Dismantling the family source of pride over an excuse as flimsy as boredom? Neither could believe their ears.

Lord Lambert must have known the game was up. When he twisted around to face them, his shoulders were slumped and his expression decidedly downcast. "Please, keep that news to yourself. I took great care to prevent my wife from discovering the truth. She'd be mortified if she knew what I'd done."

"But how have you kept such a thing from her?" Benedict asked, echoing Rex's thoughts.

"She has little interest in racing beyond ordering a new dress and hat for Ascot." Lord Lambert's gaze shifted to the tray of decanters and glasses.

Rex took the hint. He told the men to sit while he poured Lord Lambert a drink. Lambert's hand shook when he took the glass, but he managed not to spill on himself.

"I hate to pry, but given the gravity of the situation, I feel I must. Better you tell us the truth so we can help, rather than facing the police constable on your own. We heard the news of the stolen necklace in Dublin. Was it really taken, or did you use that excuse to cover up for something else? Something with Count Vasile?"

Lord Lambert spluttered his drink. His eyes grew wide, and he stared at Rex and Benedict. Rather than launching into a confession, he laughed. It was low at first, but soon picked up speed until the man was wiping his eyes.

"How strange is life that I wish it was as you said! That would be preferable to the truth. I tell you again, I never met the count. As to the theft, that was also real. Although, the joke was at the thief's expense."

"I... don't understand," Rex stuttered. He glanced at Benedict, but he was none the wiser. "What was the joke?"

Lord Lambert grasped his glass tight in both hands and stared morosely into it. "The necklace was a fake. I sold the real one a year ago to pay off our debts. Like the horses, I kept the truth of our financial situation from Lillian. When I heard her blood-curdling scream in the hotel, I feared the worst. But when she told me what was gone, I barely kept myself from howling with laughter. The thief took a fake, but I was the only one who knew the truth. Insurance paid for the loss, and I ended up making money off the necklace twice."

"Didn't you worry they'd find out about the earlier sale?" Rex asked.

"I was careful. I got my valet to order a duplicate. Then, I unstrung the pearls, and sold them off a few at a time. Enough time had passed before the theft, that no one made a connection. I slipped my valet an extra payment for his troubles and he kept quiet."

"And Lady Lambert?" Benedict asked. "You're sure she didn't know?"

Lord Lambert raised his gaze to meet Benedict's eyes. "I wouldn't be standing here if she did, as she'd have had my head. The only two people who knew were me and my valet."

Despite Lord Lambert's convincing answer, Rex felt a

niggle of doubt. What if Lady Lambert had discovered the truth and arranged for the theft to cover up the loss?

He didn't know if he was on to something, or wandering further off track. Jewellery theft had nothing to do with spying, unless the money went to cover illicit activities. Once again, what seemed like a clue had only brought along more questions.

Chapter 19
Dora plays croquet

D ora kept the smile pasted to her face until Rex left the room. As soon as the door closed behind him, her shoulders slumped. That had been awful, and just short of an unparalleled disaster.

How odd it seemed to remain on the opposite side of the room. She'd pushed Rex away when she longed to pull him close. The behaviour was entirely out of character for her, and had required her full attention to execute. Even then, Rex had taken notice.

Dora trudged to her dressing table and sank into the chair. The mirror showed a pale-faced woman whose wan complexion stood in stark contrast to her dark hair. Dora grabbed a cloth and got to work removing the extra make-up. Scrubbing brought colour back to her cheeks, but her eyes still lacked lustre.

She'd known staying away from Rex wouldn't be easy. However, the difficulty of the challenge only underscored why it was necessary. Her romantic sentiments were a distraction, plain and simple. With Benedict watching her every move, she couldn't afford to make even a minor mistake.

She gazed into the eyes of her reflection and offered a silent pep talk to cheer herself on. Theodora Laurent never backed down in the face of difficulty. She recalled a phrase her mother had taught her when she was still a girl.

"The best protection a woman can have...is courage," her mother had said. "Do you know who came up with that phrase, my darling child?"

Ten-year-old Dora shook her head, making her blonde ringlets swing in the air.

"Elizabeth Cady Stanton. Look her up in the morning, as I'm sure you'll like her. She fought for the rights of women in my homeland."

"Can she come here and fight, too?" Dora had asked.

"She's dead and gone, so someone else will have to pick up her baton." Her mother had cupped her chin. "Maybe that someone will be you. Courage is one thing you have in spades."

"I've got more courage than Will or Benedict," young Dora had declared, earning a laugh from her mother. "That's why I rip my skirts so often. Since courage is so important, you and Nanny should stop chastising me for ruining my clothes."

Her mother had shaken her head at her brash child. "Courage comes in many forms, darling. Sometimes the hardest choice requires you to walk away, or to turn your back on a path. Jumping every time your brothers bait you doesn't make you brave so much as foolhardy. Weigh situations with your heart and your head, and then do whatever is required. Do you understand?"

That night, Dora had nodded her head, even though it was a lie. She had been too young then to comprehend what her mother was telling her. Now she was older and wiser. The circumstances of the weekend required cool heads and steady hearts. Clinging to Rex's arm made her heart do the opposite.

The memory of that childhood conversation brought Dora some measure of comfort. It was enough to bring her attention back to her task, which wasn't sitting at her dressing table staring off into space.

Dora wanted a chance to speak with Sir Elmer and Ida Dixon. If she hurried, she could catch them in their rooms and invite them to join her outside. The Murphys were busy with Harris, and Lord Lambert was Rex's assignment. With any luck, Dora would have at least half an hour without any interruptions.

She removed her wig and hair pins, powdered her nose and applied fresh lipstick. All she had left to do was put her jewellery back on and slip into her normal clothing. She spotted her rings sitting in a small crystal bowl near the mirror, but her earrings were nowhere to be found. She cast her mind back to when she'd removed them. She'd been in a rush to get ready before Cynthia showed up with her costume kit. Dora had a vague recollection of placing the diamond studs on the dressing table, but nothing beyond that.

To be safe, she had a quick check between the bottles of perfume and pots of rouge. She even checked the floor underneath, but there was no sign of them. Cynthia must have put them in with the costume make-up by mistake.

Or, Mews made off with them. That cat was always causing trouble.

Dora selected a new pair from the travel case in the table drawer and moved on to changing her clothing. Her morning choice of wardrobe served her haste well again. She tied the sweater coat belt around her waist and rushed out the door.

Miss Dixon's lodgings were across the hall from Dora's. She called for Dora to come in. Dora opened the door wide enough to stick her head inside the room. Like herself, Ida had dressed for the day and sat by the fire, flipping through a magazine.

"Please tell me you've come to keep me company," Ida pleaded. "I've read this fashion periodical cover to cover twice already. Another time through and I'll have it memorised."

"I can do you one better," Dora answered. She motioned for Ida to get up. "The sun is shining and I've got permission to escape as far as the lawn. Would you care to join me for a round of croquet or tennis match?"

Ida cocked her head to the side and got a cheeky grin on her face. "Will there be cocktails?"

"Oh, I should think so!" Dora answered. "Although we should probably limit our consumption until after we've faced our inquisition with the police constable. From what I've understood, he's got the Murphys and the Lamberts above us on his list."

Ida tossed her magazine aside and leapt from her chair. "I don't know why I asked you that, given I'd come along regardless of what you proposed. That said, I'll take the extra incentive. Let's go." She ducked into her dressing room to grab something to keep her warm and emerged with a thick woollen sweater similar to Dora's.

The pair of women made one more stop to collect Sir Elmer and then wound their way around to the rear staircase.

"No point tempting fate by walking past the drawing room now. That's where the constable has set up shop." Dora guided them through the maze of hallways until they arrived at the doors to the terrace.

As requested, the housekeeper had arranged for a table of food and drinks. Dora spied her favourite cucumber, cream cheese, and mint sandwiches, but resisted the temptation. Seated barely a stone's throw away were the dowager duchess and Lady Lambert. Dora had no desire to cross swords with Lady Lambert so early in the day.

She looped her arm through Ida's and, after a quick wave of

hello, led her down the stone stairs to the stretch of green lawn. This late in the year, the lawn no longer bloomed with the rich, green tones of summer. But the Ducklington gardeners ensured it nonetheless remained a welcoming expanse. Further along the hedge-lined stone paths marked the start of the formal gardens. Here, there was space aplenty for the typical outdoor party games.

Sir Elmer pulled a cigar from his breast pocket and waited for a footman to provide a light. "Given our uneven numbers, I'll let you two ladies have the first match of the day. I'll join in when one of the other men catches up."

"Oh, that reminds me!" Dora grabbed a mallet from the bag and spun around to face the others. "We've had an unexpected arrival. Lord Clark — Kenworthy, that is — showed up on our doorstep this morning, and I do mean that literally."

"Lord Clark is here?" Sir Elmer brightened at the news. "Old chap never could stand to be left out, no matter what we were doing. Haven't seen hide nor hair of him since Ireland, either. While I'm happy to have another friendly face in the group, how'd you get the police to give their approval?"

Dora shrugged her shoulders. "You know how Clark is. When he gets his mind set on something, heaven help anyone who gets in his way. He tossed out the Duke of Marlborough's title and mentioned he'd been weekending at Blenheim, and that was that."

Ida was gobsmacked, but Sir Elmer threw back his head and laughed. He sobered up soon enough. "I'm sure I can count on Lord Clark to raise a glass with me tonight in memory of Vasile. We had some hair-raising adventures in Ireland, the three of us."

"Clark mentioned something of the sort. He took the news hard, as well." Dora glanced away to give Sir Elmer a moment to gather himself. She'd planned to pump him for information about Vasile, but a new idea came to her mind. "Clark is staying in the Birch room, if you wanted to catch him for a private moment to reminisce. I daresay we'll have few opportunities to speak privately now that the police are here." Dora motioned to the guard stationed in the corner of the terrace. "Do you want me to ask a footman to show you the way?"

Sir Elmer turned first to his companion before giving Dora a reply. "Would you mind terribly if I disappeared for half an hour?"

Ida stepped away from the bag of mallets and hurried to his side. "Don't you worry about me. Theodora and I can enjoy girl talk until you get back. You'd be bored stiff if you stayed." She patted his arm and sent him on his way.

Dora waved for Archie to come over. "Please escort Sir Elmer to the Birch bedroom and wait outside until he and Lord Clark are ready to join us." To Sir Elmer, Dora added, "Archie will make sure you don't get turned around on your way back."

Archie would do that, but he'd also keep his ear to the door while Sir Elmer spoke with Clark. This was even better than her original plan. Sir Elmer might let slip all kinds of information while he and Clark were on their own.

Dora handed Ida her mallet and chose another for herself. "Don't worry about keeping score or lining up your shots. We'll knock the balls around enough to keep Lady Lambert and Lady Rockingham from coming over."

"I like the way you think, Theodora," Ida said. "If the circumstances weren't so darned awful, I'd say this was my dream weekend."

"Come now, you can't mean that," Dora replied. "I'm sure Sir Elmer has escorted you to many places."

"Fewer than you'd imagine. We haven't been seeing each other for very long, and we have spent most of that in London."

"Did you two meet in London? Club 43, perhaps, or one of the underground jazz clubs?"

"We met on the ship back from Ireland. I'd been on a visit there, staying with a cousin, and was on my way home. Sir Elmer had been at the wedding, as you've heard. We met in the ship's lounge and hit it off."

"Ah, the invisible hand of fate. It put you two in the right place at the right time so you could find love."

"Love, and high crime," Ida said, earning a gasp from Dora. "Elmer was due to stay in Dublin for another week, but after a slew of high-profile thefts at the major hotels, he decided to come straight home. As sad as it is to say, I owe my good luck to a criminal."

Dora could hardly believe her ears or her luck. "Did you hear Lady Lambert was one of the victims?"

"What? No!" Ida covered her mouth with her hand.

It took Dora a moment to figure out Ida was laughing.

"I'm so sorry. I shouldn't laugh, but she's just so..."

"Horrid?" Dora finished the sentence.

"Yes, exactly. I don't wish anyone ill, but at the same time, I can't help but feel she may have reaped what she sowed. The papers speculated the thief might be a member of the upper crust. Whoever it was moved around Dublin's fanciest hotels with no one the wiser." Ida stopped to tap a wooden ball under a line of hoops. "Enough about my gossip. Can we talk about your adventures? Is it true you once had dinner with a Romanov?"

"We did more than have dinner. Come by my room and I'll show you the fur coat he gifted me after a night on the town." Dora carried on with stories of her past, peppering in more questions about Ida's relationship with Sir Elmer along the way.

When Rex and Benedict joined them, Dora's mind was still circling around the stories of the jewel thief. Was it possible they had the motive all wrong? She'd been sure Vasile was in

England for a mission, but perhaps the thief struck before he could execute his plan.

If that were the case, she was desperate to hear what Rex and Benedict had learned from Lord Lambert. But it would be a long day of idle chatter before they all had the chance to put their heads together again.

Chapter 20
The roaster

C louds rolled in around mid-afternoon, casting strangely shaped shadows over the patchwork fields of the Cotswolds. From his bedroom window, Rex no longer saw the stone walls delineating one field from another. Large black swaths hid the finer details of the landscape from his sight.

The investigation into Count Vasile's murder was in a similar state. Their sleuthing had illuminated certain areas, but others remained unclear. The line between truth, lies, and irrelevant information shifted with the wind.

Rex was amazed they'd got away with Harris masquerading as the constable for so long. It was testament to how little most people knew about police procedures. He suspected that a real investigation would involve many more people, invasive searches, and trips to the station for questioning.

Eventually, his guests would ask questions. They needed to wrap up their search for the killer before the weekend was done. But it was already Saturday. Come Sunday evening, Mr Murphy would need to return to London for work. Sir Elmer and the Lamberts might linger longer, but Rex couldn't count on that.

Rex closed the curtains and left his room to join Dora and Harris in the library. His footsteps made no sound on the thick carpet running along the hallway. Even the sound of his door clicking shut garnered no reaction from the inhabitants of the nearby rooms. Rex understood at that moment how easily someone had snuck into Vasile's room, with no one the wiser. The house was full of guests and servants, yet he felt entirely alone.

His morose sentiments stuck with him all the way to the library. The two people waiting inside did little to lift his spirits. Dora had her back to him. She stopped warming her hands in front of the fireplace long enough to glance over her shoulder and call a hello. Harris sat in a nearby wingback, with one leg crossed over the other. He had his notepad open and was busy reviewing his notes.

"Please tell me you spotted an inconsistency in someone's story, or better yet, got a full confession," Rex said to get Harris's attention.

"I'm afraid not. If such a miracle had happened, rest assured I wouldn't have waited until now to tell you both. I didn't learn anything new. How did the pair of you get along?"

"I got an earful about a series of robberies in Dublin," Dora said, answering before Rex could get a word out. "According to Ida, guests in multiple hotels suffered from theft. That puts paid to my theory that the Lamberts were somehow involved."

"I wouldn't be so sure about that." Rex chose a seat on the sofa across from Harris and patted the space beside him. Dora gave a shake of her head and stayed where she was. "You were right about the Lambert's having money problems. Lord Lambert admitted he'd pawned his necklace months earlier and replaced it with a fake. His wife was none the wiser. The theft was a blessing in disguise. Lord Lambert said he filed a claim on the insurance. He made out like a bandit."

"Literally," Harris added. "If I were a working officer of the law, that piece of information would be very interesting."

Dora crossed her arms and leaned against the mantle. "As a spy, that knowledge is still useful. Should we have need of support from Lord Lambert in the future, it will make for leverage. Write it down, anyway."

"Yes, madam." Harris mocked her with a half bow but did as she asked.

The moment of levity cleared some of the black clouds in Rex's mind. He'd discarded the theft of the necklace as irrelevant, but what if the series of burglaries was cover for something else?

The only way to find out was to raise the question. He cleared his throat to get Dora and Harris's attention.

"Is there any chance Count Vasile turned to crime to fund his ventures? Might that even have been his assignment? Don't discount the idea. From what you've taught me, there's plenty of overlap in the skillsets of spies and cat burglars."

"True as that may be, in this case, you're wrong." Dora raised a hand to stave Rex for pushing back. "I considered the same theory earlier today. Unfortunately, it doesn't fit with anything I know about the man. Yes, his work was similar to mine, but our approaches were completely different. I kept watch over him plenty of times through the years. I never caught him running along the rooftops or scaling walls. He wined, dined, finagled, or romanced his way to whatever intelligence he needed."

When Rex raised his eyebrows, Dora added, "Yes, fine, I did those things, too. But they weren't my only methods. You'd never catch Vasile wearing a servant's uniform, that's for certain... which is unfortunate, as I'd have paid good money to see that sight."

"You'll have to find someone else to indulge that particular fantasy of yours," Harris quipped.

Rex caught Harris motioning in his direction, but Dora gave a minute shake of her head. So he hadn't imagined her cold shoulder. But why? He couldn't come up with a single explanation for her sudden change in behaviour. Unless the count had meant more to her than she'd let on. Was that it?

Rex studied her surreptitiously, but it was no use. Her expression was flat and her posture unrevealing. She didn't look like someone in mourning. She was a professional at work, and nothing more.

Not much of a useful insight, but it was all Rex had. As long as they had a murderer hiding in the house, questions about future romantic encounters were irrelevant.

Harris's voice pulled Rex's attention back to their discussion. "I agree with Dora. Thefts months ago in another country smell fishy. We're too short on time to allow ourselves to be distracted by a red herring. We expected Vasile to take advantage of the weekend to conduct some sort of spy mission. There's nothing so far to disprove that theory."

"But nothing to prove it, either," Dora countered. "Still, there are worse positions to be in, so let's lay all the pieces to this puzzle on the proverbial table and see what kind of picture we can make of them. Harris, what did you learn through your interrogations?"

"I began with the Murphys. They repeated the story of the whiskey exporting venture, adding in more details about Mr Murphy's discussion with the count. Beyond that, all I got was a list of people they remembered meeting at the wedding. How useful that is, I have no idea."

Rex hadn't expected much, and that was the only reason he wasn't disappointed. "What of the Lamberts?"

"They didn't budge on their claim that they had never met

the count. The most they would agree is that potentially their paths crossed during their short stay in Dublin. However, even if that were the case, they were never introduced to the man. Having still not seen the count, they couldn't say anything more. I don't want to ask Lord Lambert to view the body."

Rex shivered at the thought. "I agree. Did you speak with Sir Elmer again?"

Harris shook his head.

Dora offered an explanation. "I sent Sir Elmer to find Clark, with the suggestion they raise a glass in memory of Vasile. They took me at my word and didn't stop there. By the time Archie alerted me to their inebriated state, the only thing to do was stuff them with bread and water and send them to bed to sleep it off."

Rex desperately wanted to laugh, but he bit his lip to hold back his mirth. Clark's presence brought both benefits and costs. They'd been naïve to overlook his potential for causing havoc, even when unintended.

Dora pushed herself away from the mantle and began pacing the length of the room. "As much as I'd like to paint the Lamberts as our killers, they aren't capable of pulling off a near perfect crime. Lady Lambert would never dirty her hands, and Lord Lambert crumbles under the first hint of pressure. So that leaves us with the Murphys and Sir Elmer. What do you think, Harris?"

"Slim pickings, but that was true from the start of this case. Since you've forced me to pick a favourite, I'll put my money on the Murphys."

"Why?" Rex asked, genuinely curious.

"He's a politician." Harris held his hands wide, as though the phrase was explanation enough.

Dora gazed skyward and huffed her hair out of her face. "If we're using that as our criteria, we should put Benedict on the list. Please tell me you have a suggestion for how we proceed."

Harris sat back again and retrieved his pen and paper. He tapped the pen against his chin while mulling Dora's question. "There's one technique we used, although I'll need help to determine how to make it work in our current setting."

Rex leaned forward. "Go on, man. What is it?"

"We called it the roaster. Idea was simple — turn up the heat on the suspects. Nine times out of ten, the true criminals attempt to run away or cover their tracks."

"And the other ten per cent?"

Harris grimaced. "Those were the smart ones. But that kind of knowledge came from experience more than anything else. No one here fits that bill. Anyway, I don't have a better suggestion. So we proceed with a roast. How do we set it up?"

Rex and Dora looked at one another first, but found no help there. Dora glanced away and Rex followed suit. The two let their gazes skim the room in search of inspiration. Almost simultaneously, they spotted Vasile's two large luggage trunks.

Dora turned to Harris. "Does anyone outside our inner circle know you've searched both trunks?"

"No, not as far as I know."

"And you still believe Vasile's killer only looked inside the top trunk, correct?"

"We have no reason to believe otherwise. You can see for yourself how large and unwieldy they are. Even Sir Elmer would struggle to move them around without making some kind of noise."

Dora rubbed her hands together. "I have an idea."

In her excitement, Dora rushed back across the room and took a seat next to Rex. Her cheeks were flushed and her eyes bright. Rex could almost feel the energy thrumming from her.

Both his hopes and his spirits rose. When Dora was like this, she was invincible.

She scooted forward until she was on the edge of her seat

and pitched her voice low. "We're going to spread the word that the police intend to pick the locks on Vasile's trunk tonight. Harris hadn't bothered with them before now because he didn't want to damage the item unnecessarily, and he didn't have the right tools to hand. Until then, everyone is to remain out of the drawing room."

Harris gave Dora an encouraging nod. "I like it so far, but won't people ask if I have a suspect in mind?"

Dora chewed her lip while contemplating the question.

Rex responded faster. "What if Harris takes a servant with him? Archie or Basel? He can take them in for questioning at the station, based on new information. In fact, that might work even better. Harris leaves with a suspect in tow, with a plan to come back with the lock picks to see if there is anything else in the trunks that might be useful for evidence."

"That would create a narrow window of opportunity for Vasile's contact to beat you to the punch. I like it!" Dora cried.

"I've roasted criminals using much flimsier pretences. And given we've got no other choice, I vote we proceed. Ring for the nearest of the twins so we can clue him in on his new role as potential murderer. I'll take the man at the gate with me, but leave the others in place. They can guard the front and rear doors from the house. You two keep watch inside."

"We won't be alone," Dora said. She rubbed her palms on her trousers. "Let's ask Benedict to help. It will do him good to see the inner workings of one of our missions, as unusual as this one might be."

Harris wiggled a finger at her, but he softened his telling off with a big smile. "You forget yourself, Theodora Laurent. In our line of work, there's no such thing as usual."

Chapter 21
The trap snaps shut

With no time to lose, the trio leapt to action. Rex rang for a footman, and conveniently, Basel was the first to arrive. While Rex explained why Basel was about to embark upon an unexpected drive through the countryside, Harris set off to update his men about their plan.

That left Dora to coordinate the rest of the plan. Her first stop was on the upper floor in the private suite belonging to Rex's grandmother. There she found Edith and Inga engaged in a fierce battle over a chessboard. The black had the advantage, but Dora knew of an unusual series of moves that would give the white pieces the upper hand. Wisely, she kept that information to herself. Neither woman would appreciate her interference.

"If you two can call a temporary truce, I have an update and a request."

Edith lifted her hand from her piece without moving it to a new position. "I'm amenable to a brief pause. Have you identified the murderer?"

Dora stopped herself from saying no automatically. "We're close, and that's why we have a plan. We're arranging an irresistible temptation and crossing our fingers that our culprit will take the bait. With luck and a fair wind, we'll have our suspect in hand before the dinner bell rings."

"I like the sound of that." The dowager pushed her chair away from the table and rose. "Tell us what you need."

"I need eyes and ears," Dora answered bluntly. Those words worked like magic at pulling Edith and Inga into her web. Those two loved intrigue as much as she did.

Dora summarised their plan to catch the killer breaking into Vasile's allegedly unopened travel trunk. Dora and Rex intended to exploit the hidden doorways and spy holes in the drawing room.

"Could the two of you keep watch up here? Archie and Percival will do their best to ensure none of the servants are around to interrupt. That said, I'll feel better knowing we've got every aspect of the house covered."

Inga and Edith exchanged weighty glances.

Surely, the two weren't going to refuse.

Inga put Dora out of her misery. "You know you can call upon us for anything. I'm sure I speak for us both when I say we'd prefer to spy on the drawing room. However, you and Rex have earned the right to the front row seats."

Dora gave her dearest friend a hug. "I'll memorise every moment so I can provide an accurate recounting later." She stepped back and reached over to take Edith's hand. "Thank you again for everything — this, the use of the house, your insights..."

Edith cut Dora off before she ran through her long list of reasons for being grateful. "I promise you, my dear, that the pleasure of being even a small part of the action is payment enough. Now, off with you. I can guide Inga to the best positions to keep watch."

Dora left the room using another one of the hidden

doorways. This one put her close to the servant's staircase, where Cynthia was waiting.

"Everything all set downstairs?"

Cynthia confirmed. "Harris made a scene when he dragged Basel out the front door and put him into his car. I noticed more than a few curtains twitching in the bedrooms on the front of the house."

"Excellent. And Rex, is he in place?"

"He's hidden behind the servant's entrance, listening and watching through the keyhole. He suggested you keep a lookout from the spy hole next to the vase on the mantle."

Dora wanted to be the one to leap out and grab the culprits, but she could see the wisdom of Rex's plan. This was his country house. No one would think twice about him knowing the location of the hidden entrances into rooms. Besides, Dora knew she'd be close to an exit in the main hallway. She'd only be a moment behind him.

"Lord Benedict? Is he coming?"

Cynthia bit her lip and shifted awkwardly. "All Lord Rex said was that he'd refused the invitation."

Dora bit back a curse. Leave it to Benedict to absent himself in the one moment she wanted him around. There was no time to argue with him, however. She'd get the full story from Rex when all was said and done. "Right, then I should spread the word now about the constable's arrest and intention to return. You go get ready to let Harris back in through the servant's entrance."

Dora hurried back into the dowager's suite. Edith and Inga had already left. Dora took a moment to check her hair in the mirror. Despite the excitement bubbling in her chest, she made sure to carefully control her expression, so it remained placid. She envisioned her role as an actress reading a part in a play. Their guests had to be absolutely convinced of Dora's relief on

Rex's behalf. The culprit was caught, the weekend saved, and everyone was safe.

She knocked first on the door to the Queen Victoria room. Lady Lambert answered after several minutes, blinking the sleep from her eyes. She was still dressed, but had obviously nodded off in the mid-afternoon languor.

"Rex asked me to provide you with an update on the investigation. The constable left shortly ago with one of the servants in tow — a recent addition to the household whose identity turned out to be fake."

"I'm not surprised in the least," Lady Lambert said with a sneer. "Good help is in short supply, especially this far into the countryside. Are we free to make plans for our departure?"

"You can, although Lady Rockingham hoped you'd stay until the morning. She's planning a special dinner as her way of apologising." Dora turned to go, but spun back as though she'd just remembered something. "You might want to avoid the drawing room for the next hour. The constable had to fetch a lockpicking set so he can get into the count's travel trunk. One was locked and we can't locate the key. We put the trunks in there until he returns to deal with it."

Lady Lambert stuck her nose in the air. "Have you looked at the hour? I realise you have no sense of decorum, but now is not the time to be gallivanting around the house. The servants will be about their duties," Lady Lambert explained, as though she was speaking to a child. She finished her sentence and then promptly closed the door in Dora's face.

Dora clenched her teeth and counted to five in her head. That woman was ghastly. No other description sufficed. One more day and she'd see the back of her head.

Fortunately, Dora's conversations with Lord Lambert, the Murphys, and Ida proceeded much smoother. They all nodded their understanding and thanked her for letting them know.

None lingered long enough for Dora to get a proper read on their reactions.

She moderated her steps until she was out of sight of the guest wing. Then, she descended the steps as quick as she dared in her black leather Mary Janes and hurried over to the door hidden behind an old suit of armour. She took great care when sliding the door open, as the entire statue moved with it.

An orange and white blur bolted from the dark depths of the hidden corridor. Dora had to bite her knuckles to keep from unleashing a blood-curdling scream.

Of course, it was none other than Rex's cat Mews. Dora still had yet to figure out how the cat made its way into the various secret passageways, given the entrances were kept closed. Now free, the cat stretched across the marble floor and got to work cleaning its fur.

Dora stuck out her tongue at the beast and then hurried into the corridor before it sought retribution.

After a few steps, she turned into a narrow stretch that ran between the library and the drawing room. A soft glow alerted her to the spyhole. Light from the drawing room beamed through the perfect circle in the wall. Dora had to stand on a concrete block to see through it, but once she stepped up, she had a perfect view of the drawing room.

Harris and his men had moved the trunks from the library to the drawing room, and left them in the middle of an open space between two seating areas. Rex's hiding spot was in the corner on the other end of the room. Dora stuck her little finger through the hole and wiggled it around, in their prearranged signal that she was in place. She pulled it out after a moment and fixed her gaze on the room.

The wait seemed interminable, even if it was twenty minutes at the most. Dora was used to entertaining herself during stake-outs, but the need to stay in one spot, coupled with the small corridor, limited her mobility. When her legs got tired, she shook them one by one.

She leaned over to scratch an itch on her left calf when she heard a noise in the drawing room. She jerked upright as though a bolt of lightning had hit her spine. Her senses magnified, and she held her breath as she moved into place.

The drawing-room door opened. Two people came inside — a man first, followed by a woman. The woman remained at the door with her attention focused on the main corridor. She pushed the door closed, but took care to leave a finger-width gap between the edge of the door and the frame. She was to be the lookout.

The man crept on silent feet deeper into the room. He went straight for the trunks and paused before them. He tried the lock on the left one. It slid open with a thud and the man sighed in relief. He made quick work of looking inside, but his relief turned to frustration when he saw the contents. It was the case half-filled with underwear and nothing more.

Dora didn't move. She and Rex had agreed not to take action until they had undeniable proof of illegal activities. Searching an unlocked case was bad manners, but not a crime.

The man glanced over his shoulder at the woman. He snapped his fingers to get her attention. She gave him a thumbs-up and then motioned for him to hurry.

This was it.

The man reached into his pocket and pulled out a pocket knife of the type issued by the army during the war. He flipped the longest knife up and shoved it into the lock, wiggling it around, not caring about the damage he was causing to the brass finish. When that effort didn't work, he wedged the blade in between the lid and the bottom of the trunk. After a few moments of struggle, he finally slid the lock enough for him to open the lid.

A professional would have asked why the constable needed a locking-picking kit for something so easily opened.

Seasoned criminals, however, these were not. The man abandoned all pretence of covering his tracks. He pulled clothes from the trunk with no regard for the expensive fabrics and pressed pleats. His frantic motions attracted the woman's attention.

"What's taking so long?" she hissed.

"The package isn't here!"

"Unfold all the clothes," she replied. "We don't know how big it is." Something in his expression must have caught her attention. She pushed the drawing-room door shut and hurried to join him.

"Let me." She nudged him to the side, and began methodically searching through the mess of men's clothing.

The man buried his face in his hands and began mumbling. Dora had to turn her head and press her ear against the wall to make out his words.

"The constable has it. Or someone else. We're doomed!"

"Yes, you are," Rex agreed. The pair froze at the hard edge of his voice. He marched from his hiding spot, leaving the hidden door open for the couple to see. With the villains caught, there was no further need to hide the secrets of Ducklington Manor.

Dora jumped down from the concrete block and scrambled to catch up. By the time she opened the door, Rex was standing guard over the trunks and the man and woman sat docilely on the sofa.

Dora circled around to join Rex. She wasn't surprised, but she wished she'd been wrong.

She'd liked Gladys Murphy. Although her time with Mr Murphy had been limited by circumstance, he'd seemed a fine enough man. The married couple seated before her were broken, perhaps beyond repair.

Dora squashed any thoughts of going easy on them. Traitors, murderers, peddler of confidential information.... Maybe even worse. They deserved no sympathy.

She crossed her arms over her chest. "If this package you sought was so valuable, why did you kill Vasile?"

Mr Murphy's head jerked up. His face drained of colour and his wife swayed in her seat. "We aren't murderers!" he insisted. "I swear on my life — on hers! Vasile's death was the absolute last thing we wanted. It's the only reason we're sitting here now."

Chapter 22
The grind of justice

Rex's elation at having identified the murderers fell as quickly as it had risen. This would not be the conversation he had imagined. When Dora took a seat in a nearby chair, he followed suit. He glanced her way, and she gave him a subtle nod to tell him to take the lead.

"The constable will be back shortly. Tell us everything now. Maybe we can help you."

Patrick Murphy leaned forward to speak, but froze without saying a word. After a moment, he looked at his wife. "It's your choice."

Gladys Murphy kept her gaze low, staring at her lap where she wrung her hands. Patrick wrapped an arm around her shoulders and pulled her tight against him, lending her his strength. That gave her the fortitude to finally lift her eyes and explain everything.

"It all started at the wedding — the one in Ireland where we met the count. Although you were too polite to raise the question, I'm sure you wondered why we attended such a high-profile event."

Rex hadn't questioned that, and now kicked himself for the mistake. The wedding predated Patrick's election to Parliament.

"The groom was my cousin. That's why we received an invitation. Ironically, we attended because we figured it would be our only chance to experience such an event. Now, I wish we'd never gone."

"Did something happen there?" Dora asked in a gentle tone.

Mrs Murphy grimaced. "No, the event went off without a hitch. We wined and dined like royalty, I saw my extended family, and we rubbed elbows with the count and Sir Elmer. The problems started after we came home. After the election," she clarified. She choked back a sob and rummaged in her pocket for a handkerchief.

Mr Murphy took over to allow her a moment to pull together. "The morning after the election, we received a telegram telling us Gladys's grandparents had gone missing. A day later, I got an unsigned letter through the post. There was a single sheet of paper inside. The message was brief but clear. Gladys's grandparents were safe, for now. But if we wanted them to remain that way, we had to do exactly as they said."

"What did they want?" Rex asked.

"They didn't ask much, and nothing which seemed illegal on the surface," Gladys rushed to explain. "They said we were to be couriers for a package — one in a line. The date and time of the meeting came later. We could hardly believe it when the next letter said to expect an invitation from Ducklington Manor for a weekend with Count Vasile. Suddenly, all those questions he'd asked me about my family made sense."

"You believe Vasile kidnapped your grandparents?" Dora was aghast. Rex felt the same.

"I don't think he was personally responsible, but can there be any doubt of his involvement?" Gladys held out her hands, begging them to understand. "I was angry enough with the man to want him dead. Until we delivered that package and got my grandparents back, my hands were tied. This is the worst possible outcome — the only man with any information is dead. The package is missing. And even if we had it, we wouldn't know where to deliver it. The count was supposed to give us the destination when he handed over the package."

The Murphy's anguish was far too real to be a show. Rex put himself in their shoes. If someone threatened or kidnapped his grandmama, he'd do whatever it took to get her back safely. He could hardly paint the couple scarlet for their choices. He asked if there was anything else he and Dora should know. The couple shook their heads in unison.

"I make no promises, but we might be able to help. Theodora and I are going to step out for a moment to discuss. I'll ask Percival to bring in tea. Take the time to pull yourselves together. You'll need a clear head for whatever happens next."

Rex rose from his chair and indicated for Dora to come with him. He stopped to pull the cord to ring the servants. He gave it three quick tugs, using the agreed upon signal for Harris and Cynthia to come. Then Rex and Dora exited the room, taking care to close the drawing-room door, but didn't go any further.

"What do we do now?" Rex asked. Although he had no desire to see the Murphys pay for their mistake, it wasn't his call to make. As the junior member of the team, he was in over his head.

"We'll help them, of course," Dora replied. "Although we'll have to play fast and loose with the truth to keep our full involvement in the matter a secret. We don't dare give them any sign we're more than the wealthy couple they see."

"How will we..." Rex trailed off as he understood what she intended to do. "You'll use Harris?"

"He and the men Audley sent up. The Murphys believe they are from the local constabulary. It won't be a stretch to say they're actually a team of detectives from Scotland Yard who were investigating the count."

"That is a genius solution." Rex got no further before Harris emerged from the doorway to the servant's staircase, with two of his men and Cynthia following in his footsteps. Rex asked Cynthia to pass along the request for tea and then gave a brief explanation to Harris. "The Murphys are inside. They aren't the killers, but they know something of use. Follow my lead."

Harris and the two men, Smith and Everly, were professional enough to take Rex at his word. Without further discussion, the group reentered the drawing room. Dora lingered near the door while Rex and the investigative trio approached Mr and Mrs Murphy.

"Mr and Mrs Murphy, I'd like to reintroduce you to Constable Harris and his men. With their permission, I can tell you they are actually detectives with Scotland Yard. They suspected Count Vasile was up to something, and reached out to me before the weekend started. They'd hoped to discover what he was doing in England. After the murder, they leapt in to play the role of police. Tell them everything you told us, and they will work with you to find a satisfactory outcome. They are your best chance of seeing your family safe, so do not hold back. Understood?"

"We understand," Patrick Murphy answered.

Rex turned to leave. Mrs Murphy reached out a hand to stop him.

"Thank you for helping us. You would have been well within your rights to turn us in for murder, regardless of what we told you."

"No thanks is needed. There is no justice for anyone if the wrong person pays for the crime."

Mrs Murphy cried again, but this time they were tears of

relief. She wiped them away with her damp handkerchief and managed a wobbly smile.

Harris thanked Rex for his cooperation and that was that. One part of their mission was done, or as done as it could be, given the circumstances.

Satisfaction at a job well executed was not top of mind as Rex and Dora made their way upstairs. They walked in silence along the hallway and then let themselves into his grandmother's suite.

Inga and Edith arrived moments later, having retreated from their lookout points when Dora and Rex returned. They walked in with broad smiles, but their expressions drooped when they saw the faces of the undercover spies.

Dora and Rex did not look happy. Far from it. Dora collapsed onto a fainting couch and sighed heavily. Rex made straight for his grandmother's writing bureau. He opened the latch, lowered the lid, and fished a silver flask from a cubbyhole. Then, he helped himself to two glasses and poured a drink for both him and Dora.

"What happened?" Edith asked after a bewildered glance at Inga. "The Murphys left their room. Not long after, Archie came to tell us you'd called for Harris. Surely that means something took place."

Dora tossed back her drink and pulled a face as the liquor burned the back of her throat. "It was a dead end. A red herring! Spy work isn't the reason the count is dead."

"But the Murphys..."

Rex held up a hand to stop his grandmother there. He laid claim to a chair and perked up when Mews crawled out from under his grandmother's bed. As if sensing his patron's need for comfort, the cat sauntered over, leapt into Rex's lap, and began purring. Rex stroked the cat's fur.

The man and cat made a picture that brought a smile to

Dora's weary face. She set her glass aside and recounted their experiences in the drawing room. By the time she finished, Edith and Inga wore matching glum expressions.

"So, you solved the mystery of why Vasile came to the UK, but you don't know who hired him, nor what their intentions are." Inga held out a hand for the flask, needing something to dull her inner turmoil. "Worse yet, Benedict turned his nose up at taking part. What explanation did he offer?" she asked Rex.

Rex pulled a face at the memory. The distracting thought bothered him enough that he stopped petting the cat. Mews voiced a miaow of dissatisfaction and tugged a chuckle from everyone in the room. With the mood somewhat lighter, Rex told them about his conversation with Benedict.

"I went to his room to ask him to join us. The invite intrigued him, but once I explained our plan, he couldn't say no fast enough. He said that had all the hallmarks of Dora's childhood antics and was bound to embarrass everyone involved. I left then because if I stuck around to argue, I was likely to end up saying something I'd regret. Maybe..." Rex stopped for a moment to glance at Dora. "At this point, berating the man might finally drive home the point that you are telling the truth."

"Until he witnesses incontrovertible evidence, he's not going to come around. Will was the only one who could talk him down once he got his back up. I never had the patience to make more than a half-hearted attempt."

Edith brushed aside that discussion. "Benedict isn't our top priority. The fact remains that we have a murderer in the house. Our suspect list shrank by two, so we've made some progress. What do we do next?"

Rex looked at Dora. Dora stared up at the ceiling as if waiting for divine intervention. When none came, she lowered her head and shrugged. "I'm fresh out of good ideas. Or even bad ideas. Tempting the Murphys out of hiding was our last resort, and I'm frankly amazed it worked as well as it did. Now, we've backed ourselves into a corner."

Rex agreed with the first part of Dora's response, but didn't follow her logic to the end. "What do you mean when you say we're in a corner?"

"We told the guests that Harris made an arrest. We can hardly leak the news about the Murphys, and even if we did, what would be the point? With a suspect in custody, Constable Harris has no ground to conduct further interviews, searches, or anything else we'd need."

"But we still have the secret passageways and spy holes," Rex argued.

"Yes, but those tools require time and opportunity. Our guests agreed to remain for dinner tonight, but plan to depart in the morning. Even if we keep watch over them all night, what are the chances they'll say something incriminating?" Dora sighed, even more heavily this time.

The urge to rush to her side and take her into his arms was overwhelming. Only the presence of the cat in his lap kept Rex in place. That, and the fear that she might reject him if he tried. He still didn't know why Dora was acting so prickly.

But he wouldn't leave her in this defeated state. She may not believe in herself, but he still had faith. He bet the others did, too.

Dora simply needed a reminder of who she was. Not Theodora Laurent. Not Lady Dorothy Cavendish. But Dora — their Dora.

"I've got a question for you, Dora," Rex said, using her name to get her attention. "And Inga, since you're both here. Tell me, is this the worst situation you've ever encountered? The one with the most dire consequences if you fail?"

Inga answered first, her instantaneous laugh telling him all he needed to know. "Absolutely not. Neither one of us is at risk of losing life or limb. As far as we're aware, there aren't any state secrets on the line. As for someone dying... well, that already happened."

Dora straightened up and joined Inga in chuckling at the dark humour of the moment. "This isn't even the worst situation I've faced regarding Vasile."

Rex took great care to keep a satisfied smile from his face. He didn't dare do anything that might undo the change in mood he'd encouraged. Instead, he did something unexpected. With no explanation, he set the cat on the floor and left the room through the secret passageway.

The women were still staring in that direction when he returned a minute later. He flipped open the book in his hand and thumbed through the pages until he found the one he wanted. "I suggest we heed the words of arguably one of the world's greatest tacticians." He gazed at the page and read the line he'd underlined. "*Opportunities multiply as they are seized. We've certainly seized every one dangled before us. If Sun Tzu is correct, we must only wait for another.*"

Dora's face lit up as a cunning smile crossed her lips. "He said something else we should keep in mind. *Wheels of justice grind slow but grind fine*," she quoted from memory. "For the next twelve hours, it is up to us to keep turning them."

Chapter 23
A final toast

The clock on the mantlepiece chimed the hour, alerting the occupants of the room that it was time to dress for dinner. Dora, Rex, and Inga retreated to their rooms to begin their preparations.

Alone in her bedroom, Dora went into her dressing room to choose an ensemble for the evening. The pink gown still hung from a hook on the wall, but she no longer gazed upon it with disgust. Vasile's untimely death had rendered the implied challenge moot.

The colour and style pulled her back into her memories, this time going further into her past. Visions of pale rose dresses with white velvet and lace trim flashed through her mind. She was ten again, standing silently beside her brothers. Nanny had polished them up and dressed them in their best for a garden party. When the other children arrived, Dora was the only girl there with a bruised elbow and scraped knee.

While the other little girls had looked at her with disdain, Dora'd had to bite back a smile. She'd earned every cut and bruise the hard way. Unlike those other girls, Dora was blessed with a mother who grew up far from British high society. Her mother spent her youth riding horses on her family farm in Virginia. Thus, Adaline Cavendish had put her foot down and declared her children would master the same skills she had — riding, caring for horses, and not being afraid to get dirty.

Those were the years when Dora had learned to climb trees like a monkey, sprint like a cheetah, and evade capture when roughhousing with Will. Only when it came time to be presentable did Lady Adaline demand they uphold the appropriate level of decorum. If the two little lordlings had dirt under their nails, that was to be expected. But when it came to Dora, the world expected perfection.

That perfection was a prison, as far as Dora was concerned. She'd begged to go to a Swiss finishing school, far from the all-seeing gaze of the upper class. War came and changed the world over. No signatures on a peace treaty could turn back the clock. Dora kept running headlong into the unknown, with Inga at her side to keep her grounded and safe. She'd morphed her image again and again since then.

The pink party dress, with its white chiffon ruffles, bore no threat. It wasn't capable of defining Dora. Its fabric was no cage. She grabbed the dress and went back into her bedroom. Standing before the full-length mirror, she held it against herself and pictured the woman she might have been if life hadn't sent her in another direction.

A knock on the door interrupted her waltz down memory lane.

"Come in," she called, assuming it was Cynthia coming to style her hair.

Rex's grandmother stole inside. When she saw Dora holding the dress, her face lit up with delight. "Oh good! You got it!"

Dora's mouth dropped open.

Edith was so busy admiring the dress, she didn't take notice of Dora's shock. "When your mother showed me the sketch, I wasn't sure you'd like it. But she insisted, saying it reminded her of the years when your family was whole. You must have thought the same thing since you brought it with you."

"I..." Dora stopped herself from saying no. She didn't want to explain to Edith about her original assumptions regarding Vasile. Although it had taken her a longer, more winding route to arrive, she'd ended up at the intended destination. "Yes, it certainly evokes a mental image I haven't seen in years."

Edith laid a gnarled hand on Dora's back and stroked it. "You were away from your family for so long. It must please you to reconnect. Despite the ups and downs."

Dora stared at the mirror and met Edith's eyes in the reflection. Theodora Laurent was the epitome of footloose and fancy free, never allowing herself to get entangled. But Dora had never wanted to be fully alone. While she was wise to resist romantic ties that might bind, she'd be a fool to cut loose from her supporters. Like Inga, Harris, Edith, and the others.

"Will you wear the dress tonight?" Edith asked, blithely unaware of Dora's train of thoughts. "If nothing else, it will rob Lady Lambert of a source of complaint. Even she can't find fault with this gown."

"I will," Dora answered in a firm tone. She'd have to send word to Inga. Catching her off guard was her second favourite pastime, but she didn't want Inga to ruin the effect. Let Lady Lambert underestimate her. Perhaps Benedict would finally remember the days when his sister had been capable of anything.

Most of all, Dora would keep everyone on their toes.

After Edith left, Dora's thoughts circled back to Vasile. What had his younger days been like? Had he, too, dreamed of adventures around the world? Or had he simply grasped at a chance to rise far above his station? Was there anyone left of his family to mourn his loss?

Vasile must have shared his secrets with someone. Where was his trusted valet? What woman held the title of latest fling? If Dora could answer even one of those questions, she'd have a much better chance of helping the Murphys rescue Gladys's grandparents.

She might even figure out the identity of Vasile's killer.

It was worth a try, long shot or not.

When Cynthia arrived, Dora was already dressed and halfway through applying make-up. Thanks to her curly bob hairstyle, she was able to eschew more elaborate coiffures.

"Be a dear and pop over to Inga's room to see if she's ready. I'd like a word before we descend to the drawing room for drinks."

Cynthia did her bidding and returned post-haste with Inga in tow. Inga got one look at Dora's dress and halted in her tracks.

"Surely you're not planning to wear—"

"It's a long story, so I'll give you the highlights. My mother ordered the dress. Not Vasile. Although that doesn't change my opinion of its inappropriateness for me, it is useful for tonight."

Inga crossed her arms and cocked her head to the side. "What are you planning, and how can I help?"

This was exactly why Dora relied so heavily on her friend. After half a decade together, they needed only the barest minimum to follow each other's train of thought.

"We should tell Mrs Murphy," Inga suggested. "I'm worried about how she'll hold up. A lifeline, no matter how tenuous, is better than nothing. And, it will be easier to pry information from Sir Elmer if there are several of us asking the questions."

Dora dispatched Cynthia on another errand, and soon her bedroom held one more. However, as Dora explained her idea, Mrs Murphy's face pinked up.

"I didn't know how I was going to make it through the meal! How clever of you to come with the thought. Patrick and I had been so focused on the larger organisation employing the count, we'd given little effort into learning more about the man himself. One question, however. Won't the investigators get angry that we're stepping on their toes?"

"I can't see why," Dora replied without missing a beat. "Anything we learn, we'll share with them. They can then chase down the leads. It isn't as though we're going to undertake some sort of undercover mission on our own."

Dora fluttered her lashes to emphasise their collective innocence. Mrs Murphy bought the act hook, line, and sinker. She left to tell her husband. When the door shut behind her, Dora and Inga shared a much-needed laugh.

"Are we ready to take on this challenge?" Dora asked her friend.

"As much as we'll ever be," Inga replied. "And if all else fails, you can explore a second career as a wedding cake topper."

"Hardy har har." Dora handed Inga a tube of lipstick. "Put some colour on your cheeks and lips, darling. For once, I need you to not fade into the background."

Dora's confidence bloomed as she descended the main staircase. Rex's words played in a loop in her head. She'd been in worse scenarios before and emerged victorious in the end. Going into any battle expecting to lose was a surefire way to guarantee that outcome.

The entire group was gathered in the drawing room when Dora and Inga made their appearance. Percival and one of the regular Ducklington footmen circulated around the room holding trays of champagne glasses.

As she made her rounds of greetings, Dora noted everyone's response to her choice of dress. For once, Ida Dixon didn't ask for the name of her designer. Mr and Mrs Murphy were so nervous, they barely held her gaze. Lady Lambert sniffed, but held back on her cutting remarks. Edith smiled brightly. Rex seemed confused, and Benedict eyed Dora with suspicion. Only Clark kept to his typical antics of fawning all over her.

At the sound of the bell, the group moved to the dining room, each pair walking side by side. Benedict cut across Rex and offered Dora his arm.

"What game are you playing now?" he hissed.

Dora's only reply was to give him her most innocent expression and pretend to not understand what he meant.

The dining room chandelier sparkled above the long table running the length of the room. Crisp white linens, crystal glasses, and polished silver gleamed on the table. The footmen lined the walls on either side of the room, waiting for everyone to be seated before serving the first course.

The men helped the women into their chairs. Rex sat at the head of the table, with Dora to his right and Benedict to his left. The dowager duchess took her place at the opposite end of the table, keeping Clark to her right, and Lord and Lady Lambert to her left. The rest of the guests sat according to their place cards.

Although it chafed to wait, Dora did her best to keep a genial conversation flowing throughout the first two courses. The guests had spent little time all together up to this point. They kept the conversation polite, discussing food and weather, and avoiding politics and crime.

When the footmen cleared the main course from the table, Dora finally raised the question of Vasile's relatives.

"Seeing everyone here to together, sitting beside someone they love, has made me think about Vasile. Sir Elmer, I don't suppose you know anyone from his family? There must be someone we should contact."

After a moment of reflection, Sir Elmer replied, "He said little about them, to the point I wondered if they had all died in the war. Our best bet will be to tell the embassy. They'll alert his heirs."

Silence lapsed again. The footmen swooped in with steaming plates of bread & butter pudding swimming in fresh cream. On the chilly autumn night, the warm dessert received a response of delight from the guests. In between bites, Gladys Murphy took her turn at extracting information.

"Although I only met him the once, hearing that Count Vasile had no family has left me with a pang of sadness. Was he such a lone entity? In Ireland, he was always in the middle of a group, capturing everyone's attention. He must have some friends beyond yourself... perhaps even one of the female persuasion."

Before Sir Elmer replied, Lady Lambert's nasally voice cut through the room.

"Must we spoil our dinner with all this talk of a dead man? It's putting me off my food."

The dowager's expression soured. If a glare could kill, Lady Lambert would have fallen face first into her dessert.

Sir Elmer demonstrated an equal lack of patience. "Many of us here counted the man among our friends. Sharing memories is a way to honour our loss, madam."

"But you aren't sharing anything," she countered, refusing to back down. "Questions of his heirs and romantic follies are hardly appropriate for this setting. I don't expect Miss Laurent or Mrs Murphy to know this, but you, Sir Elmer? You've plenty of experience dining in London's finest homes."

Dora's ire caused her vision to blur. How did Lady Lambert manage so many insults in a single phrase? Was she really that horrid, or did her rude behaviour serve another purpose? Dora kept her head down, pretending to smart from the verbal backhand, but watched Lady Lambert through a heavily lidded gaze.

Sir Elmer's face turned a shade of red, so bright one expected steam to shoot from his ears. Sensing disaster on the horizon, Clark made a timely intervention.

He tapped his spoon against his glass to draw all eyes his way. "To prevent us from ruining an otherwise lovely evening, I propose a toast, if you will allow it, Lady Rockingham."

The dowager nodded her approval. What else was there to do?

Clark pushed back his chair and stood, raising his wineglass into the air. "Regardless of how anyone feels about him now, Count Vasile is the reason we're together. Therefore, it is right that we acknowledge the man's influence on our lives, no matter how brief it was." He shifted his gaze from face to face as he spoke. "First, a toast to our hosts and their companions for opening their home to us all. Next, to those who, like me, were lucky enough to see Count Vasile at his best. Last, but not least, to those whose paths may have crossed with the count's, even if you didn't realise it at the time. May his loss remind us that life is short and we should all endeavour to make the most of whatever time we have."

"Hear, hear," Sir Elmer called out. Around the table, glasses clinked together.

Dora sipped her wine, but her mind was awhirl, all thanks to an unexpected gift from Clark, at just the right moment. She shifted her foot and tapped it against Rex's leg. When he glanced her way, she suggested they adjourn.

Rex searched her face and then nodded in understanding. "If Grandmama will allow it, we'll enjoy our cigars in the drawing room, so we might all remain together."

"Splendid idea, Rex," she said, following the unwritten script. "Miss Kay, will you accompany me on the piano? I'm sure we can find a tune we both like."

Dora lingered near the head of the table until Clark passed

within reach. She pulled him aside for a quick word. His whispered reply to her carefully posed questions confirmed her suspicions.

She let him go ahead, explaining she needed a moment to herself. When no one was left in the dining room but her and the servants, she sent a footman running for Cynthia. The maid arrived faster than expected, panting from her mad dash up the rear staircase.

"Get word to Rex. I know who killed Vasile. Tell him to meet me in the hallway in five minutes' time, and whatever he does, do not let Benedict leave the drawing room."

Chapter 24
The big reveal

What was taking Dora so long? On his way out of the dining room, Rex had turned back to catch her having a word with Clark. Clark had made his way across the house, but Dora had not.

Rex tried not to worry about her absence, but it was easier said than done. If she hadn't been so stand-offish in the last twenty-four hours, he'd have had no reason for concern. Was she up to something? Did she no longer trust him? Heaven forbid, but might there be something else going on?

Percival brought Rex a sniffer of brandy, putting a temporary stop to the whirlwind of anxiety swirling through his head. He held the tray steady and spoke in the low tone butlers used to convey private information.

"Meet Miss Laurent in the hallway in five minutes' time. Don't let Lord Benedict go anywhere in the interim."

That information did little to assuage his worry. "Did she say where she was going? Anything else?" Rex whispered.

Percival leaned forward and lowered his voice until it was barely audible. "She says she knows who is the killer."

"Oh, Percival?" Edith cried from across the room.

Percival left to do her grace's bidding. Rex stared into his glass in search of answers. Five minutes? What would she do with so little time? He glanced at the grandfather clock in the corner, noting of the position of the hands.

Benedict stood with the other men near the windows. They smoked cigars while talking about the cricket. He didn't appear to be in danger of going anywhere in the near term. That freed Rex to examine the more interesting part of the message.

Dora hadn't known the identity of the killer prior to setting foot in the dining room. Of that, Rex was sure. If she'd known, she'd have told him. That meant that she'd puzzled it out over the meal.

He didn't have her flawless memory, but he remembered enough of what they said. The only relevant part of the discussion was the bit at the end. She and Mrs Murphy had asked Sir Elmer questions. Rex hadn't missed the glances the two women had exchanged. Clearly, those questions were part of a larger plan.

But even Dora couldn't have foreseen how Lady Lambert would react. Dora's back had gone rigid with irritation every time the other woman had opened her mouth.

That left the toast... Clark's toast. It had seemed innocuous. What had he said to spark Dora's excitement?

Three minutes left to wait. Three minutes to arrive at the answer himself. Anyone capable of partnering Dora had to be as quick on their feet and just as savvy.

Two minutes remaining. The swinging pendulum ticked off the seconds. Rex replayed the toast again and again. Clark, raising his glass, acknowledged everyone and their connection to the count.

Rex let his gaze drift around the room. His grandmother and Inga sat at the piano. Miss Dixon and Mrs Murphy sang along to the popular tune. Lady Lambert pretended to be above it all.

Lynn Morrison

The men were busy being men. Everyone was so engrossed in his or her activity that no one noticed Rex standing on his own.

He excluded people from consideration — his grandmother, Inga, Mr and Mrs Murphy, and even Benedict. Dora hadn't meant to insinuate her brother was involved. She wanted him to be front and centre for the reveal.

That left a small cohort. Rex closed his eyes and shut out the ticking of the clock. In his mind's eye, he pictured Clark standing near the foot of the table, uttering his words, acknowledging them all.

He opened them again. The minute hand advanced a single space. Rex backed up slowly toward the open door and slipped into the hallway with none the wiser.

Dora descended the main staircase. Archie followed behind, carrying a hatbox. Her radiant smile revealed more to Rex than words could say.

He stood at the bottom of the staircase. She stopped on the bottom step, tall enough now to nearly look him in the eye. She opened her mouth. He held up a finger to her lips and mouthed a single word.

Her eyes widened and her smile returned, even wider than before. She reached up a hand to cup his cheek, but stopped herself midway through the gesture. "We should tell the others. Archie has the evidence, but let's save it for the end."

Rex hid the hurt caused by her unfinished gesture. They'd have time to address whatever walls she had built between them later. This close to the end, delaying made no sense.

"Would you like to do the honours?" he asked.

"Your home, so you start. I have a suggestion of how to broach the topic." Dora whispered her idea and Rex approved.

They strode in and didn't stop until they stood in the middle of the room. Inga's fingers slipped on the piano keys, resulting in a discordant chord cutting across the various conversations.

Everyone turned to find out why Rex and Dora wanted their attention.

"I have news," Rex said by way of introduction. "Constable Harris is on his way back to the house. The footman produced an alibi for the window of time during which the murderer struck."

The dowager spoke up. "Are you saying the murderer is still here?"

"In this very room."

A chorus of gasps filled the air.

"You know who it is." Clark didn't phrase it as a question, but tossed out the statement.

"I do."

"Don't make us wait for it, old chap," Lord Lambert demanded. He hustled over to join his wife on the sofa. Edith and Inga remained on the piano bench. The Murphys sought one another out, standing together near the fireplace. Clark and Sir Elmer didn't move from their place near the window.

Benedict drifted closer, as caught up in the moment as everyone else. He ended up positioned beside the wingback chair where Ida Dixon sat.

Dora remained at Rex's side. Just as before, when Rex had told the group of the count's untimely death, she studied their expressions and body language.

"Sir Elmer, shall I start with you? As Count Vasile's closest friend, we put you at the bottom of our list. Nothing about your behaviour suggested we got that wrong. So I say, for all to hear, that you are not the killer."

"Of course I'm not!" Sir Elmer blustered until Clark held up a hand to stop him.

"The Murphys quickly rose to the top of our list. They admitted to meeting the count and to discussing business plans. Perhaps it was a deal gone wrong, we thought. But later we learned this couldn't be further from the truth. They, too, are innocent of the crime."

Gladys Murphy sagged against her husband's muscular form. She fought against her fraught nerves, wanting to remain until the end.

With Sir Elmer and the Murphys cleared of wrongdoing, that left the Lamberts. Almost as one, the rest of the party gazed upon them with suspicion. Lord Lambert was oblivious, but Lady Lambert felt the heat.

She bristled. "Why is everyone looking our way? We never met the man! What reason would we have for doing him harm?"

"What reason indeed?" Rex echoed. "But your trip to Dublin wasn't without its own trials. All of London knows of your stolen jewellery. If you thought Count Vasile was responsible, who knew what you'd do?"

"Why, we'd report him to the police!" Lord Lambert insisted.

"Perhaps," Rex agreed. He let the word hang in the there, hinting there was something more to the tale. But as a gentleman, he stopped before revealing Lord Lambert's dire financial straits.

Lord Lambert flicked a glance at his wife to see if she'd noticed. She was too busy muttering her outrage at the notion to catch on to the hidden meaning of Rex's answer.

Chairs creaked as the drawing room occupants shifted uncomfortably. Rex let the tension build again. It didn't take long for everyone to resume their searches for who was left. Lady Lambert scowled at Dora, but more than a few men studied Benedict.

"Theodora spent part of the afternoon escorting Mrs Murphy on a tour of the grounds. When that finished, she left with Miss Kay to run an errand in the village. She barely had time to dress for dinner and therefore lacked the opportunity to commit the crime."

"Lord Benedict?" Sir Elmer gasped, disbelief heavy in his voice.

"Me?" Benedict shook out of his stupor. "What game is this? I drove up with your grandmother, as you well know, Lord Rex! We arrived only an hour before dinner."

"I never said otherwise," Rex pointed out. He caught a smirk sneak across Dora's face and knew she was enjoying seeing her brother squirm.

As fun as that was, it was time to bring this mystery to an end.

"Lord Benedict, you were not in Ireland when the others crossed paths with Count Vasile. Clark, Sir Elmer, and the Murphys were there. Lord and Lady Lambert must have made an impact on the man, since he added them to the list. But unfortunately for the count, the final attendees included an extra name." Rex raised a hand and pointed at Ida Dixon.

She squeaked in protest, blinking rapidly against the tears rising in her eyes. "Elmer invited me along. Tell them, darling!"

That was Dora's cue. Rex stepped back and ceded the floor.

She launched into her questions, beginning with one for Sir Elmer. "Miss Dixon told me the two of you met on the boat home. Is that correct?"

Sir Elmer kept his answer short. "Yes. I was travelling alone."

"It must have seemed a stroke of good fortune, meeting such a lovely woman. Ida said you owed your encounter to the jewel thief. She wasn't lying." Dora shifted her gaze over to the left. "Lord Clark, before this weekend, when and where did you see Miss Dixon?"

Since Clark had already answered this question once that evening, he didn't have to think long. "As I told you at the end of dinner, I saw Miss Dixon at the Grand Lodge. She was working as a housemaid."

Ida leapt up from her chair. "That's not true!"

"She's right," Dora agreed. "Miss Dixon wasn't on their staff. She was, however, masquerading as a cleaner so she could gain access to the guest rooms."

Sir Elmer blathered, "Why would she—"

Lady Lambert jerked as though hit by lightning. She raised a hand and pointed at Ida, speaking right over Sir Elmer. "You! I remember you now!"

"As well you should," Dora said. "Ida Dixon, or whatever her real name is, reconnoitred your room before making off with your famous pearls. What happened, Ida? Did Count Vasile catch sight of you as you were going in or leaving?"

To give her credit, Ida didn't succumb to Dora's interrogation. She rolled her shoulders back and held her head high. "This is absurd. You're blaming me because I'm not part of your upper class set."

"I'm blaming you because I found my missing diamond earrings in your dressing room. Along with them was a box of pound notes, Vasile's travel documents, and more of his personal items."

Archie walked through the drawing-room doorway, bearing the items in question.

Lady Lambert didn't need more evidence or information to convince her that Dora was telling the truth. "You stole from me! I'll ensure you are hanged. Where is my necklace?"

Finally, Ida's composure broke. She whipped around and shouted back at Lady Lambert. "Hanged for what, Lady High and Mighty? Stealing a string of paste beads? Your necklace was a fake!"

Lord Lambert choked and clutched his chest. His wife abandoned her fight and twisted in her seat to check on him.

Out of the corner of his eye, Rex spotted Ida Dixon making a strange move. In the confusion of more gasps and screeches for help, Ida leaned over, tugged up her skirt, and pulled a shiny silver handgun from the holster strapped to her thigh.

She didn't aim for her accusers, nor for Lady Lambert. She pointed the muzzle at the closest person.

Lord Benedict.

The man froze in place when the metal poked into his side.

Rex called for everyone to halt. "Ida, put the gun down. Don't make things worse for yourself."

Ida's face flushed with fury. Spit flew from her mouth when she spoke. "There is no worse! You'll see me convicted for thievery and murder. What's one more body count?"

She cocked the pistol without glancing down, proving she knew how to use the weapon.

"Don't move, Benedict," Dora hissed.

Rex noted the way Dora shifted her weight ever so gradually. He'd grappled with her enough times in training to recognise her intentions. Ida would never expect Dora, of all people, to be the one to take her on. Therefore, it was up to Rex to create an opening for Dora to move.

"What do you want, Ida?"

Ida shifted around until she was half hidden by Benedict's broad-shouldered form. "I want a car filled with petrol. I'll take his lordship here with me as an insurance policy. When I've got enough of a head start, I'll drop him on the side of the road."

Benedict gave a narrow shake of his head, but Rex ignored him. Benedict wasn't the one in charge here. Neither was Ida Dixon.

"Fine. Archie, bring a car around."

"Yes, my lord." Archie set the box onto the nearest table and hustled out the door.

"Move," Ida ordered, poking Benedict with the gun.

Rex kept his face impassive. He didn't want to hint what Dora was planning.

Benedict's eyes widened as the realisation set in. No one was going to save him. They were going to let this madwoman hold him hostage. Benedict never glanced at his sister, despite her being the nearest to his path out the door. Like everyone else, he'd discounted her usefulness.

Benedict lifted his right foot and moved forward one pace. Ida clung to his back, urging him onward. He repeated the action with his left, making a slow march across the room. He moved like a dead man walking.

Dora shifted her centre of balance again.

As soon as Benedict passed in front of her, she launched into action. With no hesitation, she grabbed a hold of Ida's arm and wrenched it away from her brother.

Rex was barely a half second behind. He ploughed into Benedict, knocking the man to the floor, and away from the path of the gun.

A shot rang out. Someone screamed. And then it was all over.

Chapter 25
A heart to heart

Dora's takedown plan worked almost perfectly. Rex's quick thinking ensured Benedict was out of the line of fire when the gun went off. Dora's actions resulted in the pistol pointing away from the group. It was poor luck that her own arm ended up in the way.

Mrs Murphy had been the one to scream. In her frazzled state, she'd swayed on her feet and then crumpled into her husband's embrace. Edith took one look at the blood welling on Dora's arm and decided to take command. Embodying every inch the entitled duchess, she issued orders left and right. After demanding calm, she sent everyone to their rooms, and called for a footman to carry Dora upstairs.

Harris strode in with his men and took responsibility for ferrying Ida Dixon to new accommodations. She'd soon start her time as a resident of His Majesty's prison service. Rex commandeered the box of evidence. Dora barely had time to tell him what else she'd found before Archie whisked her upstairs.

On her way out of the room, she noticed a crystal drop missing from the dowager duchess's favourite chandelier.

Nearby, the ceiling bore a new hole. However, that was a small price to pay for seeing justice served.

The only total loss was the pink evening gown. Dora told Cynthia not to bother scrubbing the bloodstains out. It had served its purpose and met a fitting end. Dora was certainly never going to wear it again. She expected Inga would take it out back and see it burned.

In the privacy of her bedroom, Inga and Edith coddled Dora until she couldn't stand it any longer. When Benedict rapped on the door, asking if he might have a moment, she said yes without hesitation. He, at least, could be counted upon to leave her be.

Unfortunately, Benedict hadn't got the message.

Dora sat in a comfortable chair in front of the fireplace. She had a woollen blanket over her lap and a cup of chamomile tea within easy reach. Thus far, she'd had no luck convincing anyone to swap the hot beverage for a sniffer of brandy.

When Benedict leaned over to tuck her blanket tighter, she smacked his hand away. "I'm fine. It's just a scratch."

Benedict reared back and glowered at her in admonishment. "You got shot, Dora!"

"It's a graze. Even calling it that is being generous. It only took two stitches for Inga to close the wound. In a couple of week's time there won't even be a scar."

Benedict was unconvinced, but he did settle back into his chair. They were alone, and for the first time in years, they weren't arguing. Well, not about anything important, anyway.

He stood up and added another log to the fire. Instead of sitting down again, he paced one direction and then the other. There was too much nervous energy flowing through his veins for him to relax right then. In her early days as a spy, Dora had been the same. Over time, she'd grown accustomed to the flooding rush of adrenaline, developing ways to manage it until danger became part of the job.

"I feel dizzy," she said.

Benedict halted in his tracks and hurried over to her chair. "Should I call Miss Kay or Lady Rockingham?"

"No, you need to sit down. All your back and forth is what's making my head ache. Either pour me a drink or spit out what you came to say."

Benedict rolled his eyes before he could stop himself, but had the grace to look abashed when she caught him. He pointed to the teacup and then sat down across from her.

"Here." He dropped a pair of diamond earrings onto the side table. "Harris asked me to see them returned."

"I'll have to apologise to Mews. I'd laid the blame for my missing jewellery on his doorstep. Is that it?"

"I wish," he mumbled, before drawing himself upright. "I'd rather debate the opposition on the floor of the House of Lords than admit what I'm about to say."

Dora braced herself. Was Benedict up to his old antics? Wasn't it enough that she'd identified a murderer and thief? She bet he didn't know she'd found the key information necessary for rescuing an elderly couple. Not to mention, she'd saved her brother's life. What more did he want from her?

"I've been a complete and utter fool."

Dora blinked. That was not what she'd expected.

"You told me. Rex told me. Harris told me. Lady Rockingham hinted at the matter. Even our father told me to trust the process. And yet, I remained blind to your abilities. Sheer pig-headed stubbornness is the only explanation I can offer, weak though it is."

Dora crossed her arms, taking care to avoid the bandage.

"Aren't you going to say anything?" Benedict asked after a stretch of silence.

"No. You're doing just fine on your own. Pray continue, dear brother."

Benedict huffed. "I suppose I deserve that. You must hate me now."

"Hate is a powerful emotion. Deplore might be better. It hints at a chance of redemption." Dora unfolded her arms and tapped her chin. "What might you do to earn my faith again? This will be an entertaining list to compile while I'm stuck being an invalid. I'm sure Inga and Edith will have a few recommendations."

Benedict threw up his hands. "You are incorrigible. You won't even let me apologise properly!"

"Given how long it took you to see reason, and, dare I say, a truth as evident as the Cavendish nose on your face, you can spare me a few moments of levity."

Benedict dropped from his seat to kneel beside her chair. He took her hands in his and looked her in the eye. "You saved my life, Dora, and risked your own in the process. All this time, I'd been fooling myself into believing you were playing games. It was easier to do that than to accept that your spoke the truth about your capabilities."

Dora's icy heart thawed. Instead of bringing joy, it released pain. "Why? Yes, I disappeared for the last few years, but as far as you knew, I was mourning my husband. When I returned to London, why were you so intent on thinking the worst of me?"

Benedict sat back on his heels and leaned against the chair legs while contemplating Dora's question. "Despite what you see on the surface, life after the war hasn't been easy. Will was gone. You abandoned us. Father threw himself into his work in the government. I found myself wholly unprepared to play the role of only child. Mama suffered greatly, Dora. She put on a good front for the rest of the world. Sometimes I'd find her sitting in your room, or Will's, late at night. When I saw you masquerading as an international party girl, I... broke, I guess. It was far, far easier to detest you than to ask questions about your intentions."

Dora weighed his words. The blunt edge led her to believe he spoke honestly. She put herself in his shoes. Would she have acted any differently if their roles had been reversed?

"I'm sorry, too. I was so focused on escaping the yoke of societal pressures, I never stopped to think about how that weight fell on you. Thank you for taking care of Mama. For being there when I wasn't."

Benedict shifted his weight forward and rose from the floor with a groan.

"Where are you going?"

"To get the bottle of brandy. If you promise not to rat me out to your nurses, I'll pour us both a glass."

Dora mimed sealing her lips, earning a chuckle from her brother. He crossed the room and busied himself with the drinks. Dora noted the droop in his shoulders. He was exhausted. So was she. Fighting one another took more effort than either could muster. Perhaps it was time for a fresh approach.

She murmured her thanks when he passed her a glass. He'd limited her pour to a finger of liquid, but she didn't complain.

"So..." he said after he sat back in the chair. "Miss Kay assists you? Does she also have special skills?"

"Poison and sharpshooting are her specialties," Dora said in the same tone others used to announce their interest in knitting and drawing. "You already know Harris is an ex-officer. Archie and Basel are better thieves than Miss Dixon. Their sister... well, let's just say she has her own story to tell."

Benedict marvelled at her words. "This strange team of individuals, plucked from various walks of life, and all of them working in service to you."

"Not to me," she said, correcting him. "With me. I'd be nothing on my own. You have only to look to Count Vasile for an example of how that story ends."

"You always excelled at drawing people to your side. Will worshipped the ground you walked upon, even though you led him into trouble more often than not. The servants, some of our nannies, even the groundskeepers. You weren't exaggerating when you said you'd built your skills since childhood." Benedict sipped his drink. "And Lord Rex. We can't leave him out. He is the most important one of all."

Dora nearly choked on her drink. "Why would you say that?"

"Because he is your Will."

"My what?!" Dora stared, uncomprehending.

"Perhaps it is more obvious to me since I was the outsider, but you and Will operated in lockstep with one another. There were times when I was sure you could read one another's minds. You and Rex have that same wordless understanding. Think about tonight. I still don't understand how you two coordinated my rescue."

"I—" Dora stopped there, suddenly speechless. She'd acted on instinct, knowing Rex was nearby. Her trust in him had been so absolute, she'd been oblivious to it.

"You and Will were unbeatable as a team. I should know since I played the opponent more than anyone else. Mark my words, you and Rex will be the same. I don't know how you did it, but from what I've seen, there's no better man for the job."

Benedict's comment rang like the dinner gong through Dora's head. The echoes reverberated, knocking her misconceptions and foolish worries aside. Rex had never been her weakness. Even when she'd pushed him away, he'd stood fast.

She had to go to him, to explain, to beg his forgiveness.

She tossed the blanket aside and shoved her feet into the slippers lying on the floor.

"Where are you going?" Benedict asked.

Dora raised her hands to stop him from following. A spike of pain shot up her left arm and made her wince. "Stay here. Please. I need a moment."

Benedict got halfway through a retort before he bit back his words. "Go."

And so she did.

* * *

Dora turned to the wall where the latch to the secret door hid in the wallpaper pattern. Within seconds, she was hurrying along the secret passageway, praying Rex would be alone in his room.

And that he'd forgive her.

In her haste, she didn't bother to knock. She burst into his room to find him in a state of undress. Wearing only his trousers and an undershirt, he yelped when she strode into his private domain.

Dora didn't care. She kept going until there was no space between them. She threw her arms around his waist and rested her head against his chest. His heart thudded, beating as rapidly as her own.

"Not that I'm ungrateful for this moment, but can I ask what brought this on? Does it have something to do with whatever has been bothering you the last two days?"

"You noticed?" What was she asking? Of course, he had noticed. She'd trained him to take note of behavioural changes. The choice to give her space to work through her issues, however, had been his own.

Benedict had been right. It burned that he spotted the truth before she did.

Dora pulled away from Rex, forcing her arms to loosen their hold. Despite the months of light touches and come-hither looks, this was the longest and closest they'd ever embraced.

Not to mention Rex's state of partial undress.

This wasn't how she'd meant for their conversation to go.

Dora took one step back and then another, but halted her progress there. The pair were still within hand's reach of one another.

Rex picked up his discarded shirt and shrugged it on, but he didn't bother with the buttons. "Do you want to sit down?" He spotted the white bandage wrapped around her upper left arm. "What am I saying? You're injured. Here." He pulled the chairs closer together and motioned for her to take a seat.

For once, Dora didn't know how to begin. She had long since mastered the art of disassembling. Truth-telling remained annoyingly beyond her skills. Rex gave her an encouraging smile, but still the awkward silence rang through the room.

She'd done this. Before this weekend, she and Rex had shared secrets, faced danger, and danced around their burgeoning romantic feelings. More the fool she'd been to have ever compared this with her ancient youthful dalliance.

Rex's patience ran out before she found her tongue. "Whatever it is, you can tell me. Is it that you're leaving? Is that why you pulled away? Have you come to say goodbye?"

The waver in his voice hinted at the hurt he felt.

"I had a history with the Count."

Rex shook his head at the sudden change in conversation. "I know, but you don't owe me the details. They're irrelevant now."

"I wish they were," she mumbled. She bucked up her courage and carried on. "It was shortly after the war ended. I was still green, in matters of the heart if nothing else. I tumbled head over heels."

"It ended badly?"

"Less than it should. He was on a hunt for a new British spy. I was a casual dalliance — a way to fill the empty hours of his mission. Fortunately, I discovered the truth about him before he uncovered my identity. I deluded myself into viewing the episode as a learning opportunity. I remembered the ways he used his charm to distract me. Much of who Theodora became, I owe to him."

"I see."

But he didn't see. He couldn't, not until Dora told him the rest.

"My arsenal of allure became protection for my heart. So long as I was in control, no one would ever take advantage of me again. Partnering with Inga, Harris, and the others carried no risk. But then you came along."

"Technically, you brought me into this," Rex reminded her.

Dora chuckled. "Yes, I did. I didn't realise it at the time, but I've been treating you the way the count treated me."

"No."

"Yes, I did. It's okay, I can admit it."

Rex shook his head. "Saying it aloud doesn't make it true, Dora. As the one on the receiving end, I can tell you that nothing you've said about your past rings familiar to me now. Yes, you've tied my tongue and my mind in knots more times that I can count. But you also acted as my mentor. You told me everything, even your deepest secrets. You trained me in your ways. When I stumbled, you picked me up. This weekend, we acted as partners. Does that sound like the way Vasile treated you?"

Dora scrunched her brow. She searched for the weakness in his logic, but found none. He wasn't flattering her. Looking back, she remembered those same moments, just as he'd described them.

Rex held out his left hand, palm facing upward. It was a silent, but unmistakable invitation. Dora laid her right hand on it, barely letting their skin touch.

It wasn't enough for Rex. He set his other hand atop, cradling her lithe fingers in the heat of his palms. He rested his gaze upon her face until she lifted her head enough to look him in the eye.

"I don't know what else you came to say, but I can guess at where this is going. Hear me out instead. I have no regrets about the time we've spent together. Before Freddie died and I showed up on your doorstep, I was little more than an aimless wanderer. You brought direction into my life. You helped me find my purpose, and for that, I will always be grateful. If the time has come for us to part ways, I won't hold you back. But please, don't cheapen the memories I treasure so deeply."

Then he leaned forward, and for once, he was the one to kiss her on the cheek.

He loosened his hold on her hand. Fear shot up Dora's spine. This was wrong, all of it. Letting him go would be the greatest mistake of her life.

She slid her hand forward and wrapped her fingers around his wrist. His head snapped up and his eyes searched her face.

"I didn't come to say goodbye. I'm here, asking if you want me to stay."

Chapter 26
The partnership is official

Rex pulled his Rolls-Royce to a stop in the alley behind Lord Audley's stately London home. He turned to his passenger before switching off the car.

"You're sure about this?"

Dora tugged on the brim of her cap, pulling it lower to better shadow her face. "Pray tell, darling, what reason could I possibly have to say no?"

A dozen sprang into Rex's mind, not the least being that it marked a monumental change in her way of working. It certainly wasn't in his best interest to remind her of that, especially not now. Not when he was on the brink of getting more than he'd ever dreamed.

"Nothing at all — that was a test to see whether you're paying attention. You passed with flying colours."

"I always do." Dora trailed her fingertips down his cheek before reaching over to open her car door.

Rex switched the car off and followed suit. They met in front of the rear gate to Lord Audley's property. Dora pulled a key from her pocket and made quick work of the lock. Inside, she took the lead through the garden, hurrying at a brisk pace.

They'd returned to London that morning, on the pretence of conducting their last minute Christmas shopping. In between a spending spree at Fletchers department store and pre-dinner drinks, they'd scheduled a stop in at Lord Audley's.

The black earth of empty flowerbeds lined the path. Bare tree limbs stretched like fingers, threatening to catch their hair if they ventured off the straight and narrow. Thanks to the unseasonably cold temperatures, Rex's breath hung in the air as he huffed to keep up with Dora's speedy pace. This close to the winter solstice, they didn't have to wait until midnight to have an adequate cover for their nocturnal visit. Despite the utter darkness, it wasn't yet time for supper.

Rex shivered inside his wool coat and pretended it was due to the cold. Spies weren't permitted any tics that might give away their genuine sentiments. Nonetheless, he was nervous. Come to think of it, Rex's anxious state was bog standard for a visit with the spy master. He hadn't yet grown comfortable bearing the weight of the man's searching stares.

Dora basked in them. Perhaps in a few years' time, he would as well.

That thought warmed him better than any fire would.

Side by side, the pair stepped onto the stone terrace, taking care to remain in the shadows. Dora peeked through an opening in the curtains before giving Rex the okay to proceed. He opened the library door and strode in, doing his level best to mimic Dora's confident way of entering a room.

Lord Audley lounged in a velvet upholstered chair beside a roaring fire, wearing a thick sweater with patches on the elbows. He was the picture of a typical English gentleman, with bookshelves and British scenery in the background.

If one looked deeper, they'd uncover a cunning mind and master of strategy.

Audley took off his reading glasses with one hand and closed his book with the other. "You're earlier than I expected."

Dora flounced in and unbuttoned her coat. She draped it over a chair, laid her hat on top, and then took a seat on the sofa. She patted the space beside her, motioning for Rex to join her. "I aim to keep you on your toes. It helps you stay young, or so I've heard."

Lord Audley gave her a dry look. "Given the amount of grey hair you've caused me over the years, you'll have to rediscover the fountain of youth to balance the scales."

Seeing the two of them banter as usual soothed the last of Rex's nerves. It was a reminder that he had nothing to fear from Lord Audley.

Bolstered, he waded into the conversation. "How did the rescue operation in Ireland go?"

"Without a hitch, thanks in large part to your tenacity at identifying Count Vasile's killer. If Miss Dixon had left Ducklington with her ill-gotten gains, we'd have had little clue where to start the search. Fortunately, the box of money included the delivery address. Smith, Everly, and Higgins accompanied Mrs Murphy when she delivered the package to its intended destination. At a discreet distance," he added.

"From there, they had only to follow the money, in the most literal sense of the word," Dora said. "Mrs Murphy has her grandparents back and you've got a ready-made pot of intrigue to investigate. It's Christmas morning all around."

"I don't know that I'd say uncovering a nest of vipers is a gift, but better to know of problems before they're looming large on the horizon. Now, what have the two of you done over the last few weeks?"

"We've remained at Ducklington and done nothing at all, exactly as you ordered." Dora fluttered her lashes to emphasise her innocence.

It did not fool Lord Audley. He switched his gaze to Rex.

"She's telling the truth," he protested. "Being away from the spotlight of high society has been a blessing in disguise. We've been to church with Grandmama, had drinks with my childhood mates at the pub, and even perused the crafts on display at the annual village Christmas fair."

"We've also taken advantage of the extensive terrain to sharpen our physical skills," Dora finished. "Between matching wits with Lady Edith and taking part in the weekly pub quiz, we've exercised our mental acuities as well. Come January, we'll be in prime condition to take on our next challenge."

"We?"

Rex froze. Dora had casually dropped the word into her answer. Lord Audley was far too wise to her ways to let it slip by without comment.

"Yes, *we*." Dora squared her shoulders as though preparing for battle. "I am fully aware that partnerships are far from normal in our line of work, but we've proven we're a capable team."

Lord Audley's expression didn't change. He sat, unmoving, in his favourite chair beside the crackling fire. After a moment of silence, he said, "You have, indeed."

"We've dealt with particularly challenging situations. I will admit that I entered into this partnership intending to train Rex so he'd be able to work on his own. And he can," she added, tossing a reassuring smile at Rex. "After much reflection, I've reached the conclusion that we'd be better able to serve the realm by staying together."

Somehow, Dora made the speech sound heartfelt rather than rehearsed. It was why Rex had encouraged her to be the one to broach the subject.

Lord Audley crossed his arms. Was that a bad sign?

"So, this is a purely professional decision?"

"No."

"No?" Both Rex and Lord Audley asked in unison. Rex knew the answer, but he hadn't expected Dora to be so forthright.

Dora chuckled at the two men. "Don't act so surprised. When have I ever added someone to my team strictly based on the skills they bring to the table? Inga accompanied me from day one because of our friendship. Harris followed his heart. Archie and Basel spotted a chance to save themselves and their sister."

"What of Cynthia?" Lord Audley asked.

"I brought Cynthia on board because she is so very similar to me. She has an incredible ability as a forger, and desires to be recognised for that above all else. Where else in the world will she find that kind of work without the constant threat of prison?"

Rex hadn't ever thought of it in those terms, but it certainly made sense. Dora's team remained loyal to her because she was equally pledged to them.

Lord Audley, however, wasn't treading new ground. He leaned forward and looked Rex in the face. In the flickering firelight, his grey hair and moustache took on a glow and his eyes gleamed. "Lord Rex, what have you to say about this matter?"

Rex had come prepared. "Before I met Dora, I thought bravery and levelheadedness were the two greatest skills a man could develop. On the battlefield, those capabilities made the difference between life and death. While I argue I have those in spades, since returning home, I realised there is much less call for them in daily life. At least, not for someone in my situation. I'm not cut-throat enough to survive in the political world. I'm not ashamed to admit that I haven't yet developed the cunning to go off on my own, regardless of what Dora says."

"You remain with her out of obligation?"

"What? No!" Rex shook his head feverishly. That wasn't at

all what he intended to say. "You and she offered me many opportunities to leave. I choose to stay because I want to make a difference in this world, in whatever way I can. Like all the others in her inner circle, I remain by her because she takes me as I am."

"I see." Lord Audley crossed his legs. The man might as well have been carved from marble. His impassive face served him well in the halls of Westminster, but now it made Rex want to shout at him. Surely the man would not stand in their way? Rex was prepared to go to battle, if that was what it took.

He cast a sideways glance at Dora. Unlike him, she sat, cool as a cucumber. Was she indifferent to the outcome? Doubts swam to the surface of Rex's mind. He flashed back to his days of sitting outside the headteacher's office, waiting for punishment for something he and Freddie had done.

But Rex wasn't a child any longer. He was a grown man. Yet, there he sat, waiting for someone to give him permission.

Dora hadn't phrased it as a question. That's why she showed no signs of stress. Just like that, his fears evaporated into the aether.

Lord Audley gave a polite cough to clear the air. "I can't say I'm surprised. In fact, I'd been giving thought to how we can make the most of having two spies in the same place. Under any other circumstances, I'd have to turn somersaults to keep them apart. In your case, you have the perfect excuse to stick together."

"We do, indeed. I was certain you'd see the logic. However, hold tight to your plans for the moment. I've every intention of celebrating the holidays with my nearest and dearest. And on that note..." Dora leapt to her feet and retrieved her coat. She dipped a hand into the inner pocket and pulled out a long, rectangular box. "Here. We got you a gift."

Lord Audley was at a loss for words. Rex wished he'd been

more insistent when he'd asked Dora what she'd bought. She'd dismissed his question by saying it was a small token. He'd assumed she had purchased gifts before.

Audley couldn't refuse, not without offending them both. He handled the box with great care, using a letter opener from the drawer in his side table to slice through the wrappings.

Based on the size and shape, Rex expected the contents to be a wristwatch or an elegant writing pen. Perhaps even a new letter opener, despite the clear lack of need.

Audley set the paper and ribbon aside. He cradled the box the way Rex had seen men hold hand bombs on the front lines.

"It won't bite," Dora assured him in a dry tone.

Audley lifted the lid and peeked inside. He squinted at the contents, unable to make sense of them. Fully intrigued, he flipped the top open and tilted the box until they all saw the contents.

A strand of creamy white beads hung from a single hook at the top of the box. Nestled against the midnight blue velvet lining, the perfectly matched pearls took Rex's breath away. "Egads, Dora! Are those what I think they are?"

"If the Lambert family crest has come to mind, then yes, you're on the right track."

Lord Audley glanced between the box and Dora, his mouth agape. "How on earth did you manage this?"

Dora shrugged artfully and retook her seat at Rex's side. "I know a man who knows a man," she said, waving aside the question. "After I learned of what Lord Lambert had done, I asked an acquaintance for help to reassemble the set. As expected, pearls of that quality didn't pass without notice. After a few phone calls to the right people, I had them all in my possession. Honestly, restringing them took longer than anything else."

"Why are you giving them to me? I can hardly wear them."

Dora shook her head at her mentor. "I know better than to buy you something frivolous. Despite their outward appearance, those pearls are a very useful tool you can add to your arsenal. Should you ever need Lord Lambert to accommodate a request, you'll have the ideal form of payment."

Lord Audley was still chuckling when Dora and Rex took their leave.

Bonus Epilogue

Lord Audley's feet beat a steady cadence as he strode down the halls of Westminster Palace. His stern expression dissuaded passersby from calling a hello. He was a man on a mission, and no one dared to get in his way.

The faces in the portraits lining the walls bore witness to his march into the domain of the House of Lords. He didn't slow until he arrived at his destination, a heavy wooden door marked by a golden plaque.

Without knocking, he twisted the handle and walked in.

The young man sitting behind the desk in the lavishly appointed outer office leapt to his feet. He barely made it to the door to the inner office in time to announce Audley's presence.

"Your grace," he blurted.

That was all he got out before Audley stepped past him, welcoming himself into the inner domain of the leader of the House of Lords.

The leader himself sat behind a heavy wooden desk, its edge and base flourished with carved swirls and graceful curves. He glanced up from the stack of papers occupying his attention and settled his green-eyed gaze on his unexpected visitor.

"Leave us, Timothy."

The junior clerk didn't need to be told twice. He backed out of the room and closed the door with a heavy thud.

Lord Cavendish, Duke of Dorset, pushed his papers aside and focused on the man standing before him. "To what do I owe this unexpected displeasure?"

Lord Audley, Duke of Montagu, pulled out a chair and sat across the desk from his arch-rival of many years. Periodically, circumstances forced the men to overcome their differences and forge an uneasy alliance. Dora's return to England had been one such occasion.

This was another.

"England has a problem. I have a solution."

"Then why are you here?"

"Because said solution requires me to cross hard lines — ones we long ago deemed uncrossable. While I'm perfectly content sticking my neck out to save the country, in this particular case, I can't do it on my own. That's where you come in."

Lord Cavendish scoured the man's countenance for any hint of exaggeration. Lord Audley didn't even blink.

"Does this involve the government?"

"Worse."

Lord Cavendish flinched at the harsh tone. He hardly dared to say the words. "The Royal family?"

Audley nodded.

Cavendish cast a glance toward the cupboard where he kept a bottle of Scotch tucked away. No. Now was the time for clear heads. He rose from his chair and poured two glasses of water.

Lord Audley took the proffered glass, understanding the unspoken meaning. Political rivals though they might be, they both drank from the same ultimate source of power.

When Cavendish was back in his chair, Audley opened his

coat and retrieved a letter from the pocket. He passed it to the other man.

Lord Cavendish scanned the outer envelope. "This arrived through the post?"

"Yes. Before you ask, I've had no luck tracking down the sender. The paper is available at every common stationer, and the typewriter is unknown."

Cavendish flipped the envelope over and took the letter out. It was a single page, typed, with no other identifying marks, just as Audley had described.

The message was concise.

"A wolf in sheep's clothing lurks in the Royal stables. Are you game for a hunt? If so, post the following message in the classified section of the Times."

What followed was a line of gibberish.

Dora's father snorted in disgust and flicked the letter back to Audley. "This smells of poppycock, to put it politely. Surely you aren't taking this seriously."

Instead of answering, Audley opened his coat again, this time pulling out three more identical envelopes. He laid them flat on the desk.

"The first message arrived on January third. The required message ran two days later. Since then, I've repeated the process two more times. Frustratingly, I've come no closer to identifying the sender."

Lord Cavendish wiped his dismissive expression from his face. He read through the other letters. With each one, his concern mounted. By the time he was done, his brow was as furrowed as the Scottish highlands.

"Do these letters speak the truth? Did these events take place?"

"Every single one of them. All in private, with a selective list of attendees. The only way the sender could know these facts is if they were in the room, or knew someone who was. Whoever it is has the credentials to know if someone is leaking information on the Royal family."

"Surely that makes it easier to identify who is behind this!" Lord Cavendish was hardly one to dabble in intrigue, but even he could see how to structure an investigation.

"I've done everything I can within the constraints we previously agreed upon. My area of expertise has always been the lands beyond our shores. What we're talking about here is a traitor hiding in our midst. Unlike the Chanak matter, this time, I have no reason to believe a foreign government is involved. In short, my hands are tied."

"So, take the matter to the King. Let him authorise a search for these individuals, both the sender and this wolf in hiding. Why are you darkening my doorstep?"

Lord Audley sat back in his chair, crossed his arms, and waited for the answer to dawn on Lord Cavendish.

It took only half as long as he expected.

"Bloody hell. You want to propose Dora and Rex investigate the matter." Dora's father slammed his hands on the table and growled, "Absolutely not! It's bad enough you've got her traipsing around the world doing goodness knows what. Now you want to risk exposing her here, where the truth will damage us all?"

Audley didn't move. Thus far, Cavendish was acting exactly as he expected. He knew just what to say to pull the wind from his sails.

"Do you think so little of her skills? Of their partnership?"

Lord Cavendish ground his teeth. He kept silent until he had his temper under control. "There must be another way. Find it."

"Whom shall I ring? Scotland Yard? You think the King will be more amenable to having a corps of commoners listening at the doors and windows of Buckingham Palace?" Audley watched the other man's hands clench into fists. "We swore to defend the throne at all costs. Dora and Rex have done so as well. They were brave enough to face the enemy head-on in battle. Surely they can acquit themselves equally well when conducting manoeuvres in London's ballrooms."

"Will you give their names to the King?"

"No, I won't go that far. It isn't in anyone's best interest. Someone in the Royal household is watching their every move. I won't risk him doing something that might give them away."

"Harrumph." Lord Cavendish rocked back in his chair, causing it to creak ominously. "You've tied my hands."

"The sender has tied both our hands," Lord Audley corrected.

"Fine. I will lend you my support on one condition."

"Name it."

"You give Dora and Rex the choice of whether to take on this assignment. Don't back them into a corner. I fear this will be far from straightforward."

Lord Audley barked a laugh. "Old chap, you are so right and yet so wrong. The level of difficulty will be the number one reason Dora will leap at the chance."

Lord Cavendish buried his face in his hands and groaned. "I should have tied her to a chair as a child and only released her into the bonds of matrimony."

Lord Audley gave his rival an apologetic smile. "Despite sharing no blood or other bonds with Dora, I've had the same ill luck in my efforts to rein her in. From the moment she took her first steps and said her first words, you were a goner. We all were." He lifted his water glass into the air. "God save the King."

Lord Cavendish clinked his glass against Lord Audley's and then added a toast of his own.

"God save Dora… and us all."

* * *

Dora and Rex will be back in Autumn 2023 with **Double Cross Dead**.

England, 1923. Love is in the air and all eyes are on Windsor Castle, where the royal family is celebrating a new royal engagement.

When party invitations are sent to only an elite few, Dora and Rex's invite comes with strings attached.

There's a traitor hiding within the prince's inner circle. Dora and Rex are assigned to uncover the turncoat.

Their sole lead is a tip from an anonymous informant. To get the clue, they must meet him privately during the engagement bash.

But, when they show up at the secret rendezvous, instead of a clue, they find a dead body and their friend Clark holding the murder weapon.

Has Clark turned traitor or was he framed? Dora and Rex work double-time to clear their friend's name. But can they identify the real killer before Scotland Yard's leading investigator puts Clark away for life?

Order your copy of Double Cross Dead now on Amazon.

Want to keep updated on my newest books? **Subscribe to my newsletter** for book news, sales, special offers, and great reading recommendations.

Historical Notes

When plotting this book, I sought reasons why a foreign spy might operate on the English shore in 1922. After skimming through a few historical websites, I set my sights on the Irish state.

From 1919 to 1921, the British and the Irish battled in the Irish War of Independence. Although officially settled in December 1921, with the signing of the Anglo-Irish treaty, the bloodshed didn't end there. Guerrilla wars rarely have a tidy end date.

By late 1922, the time period in which this story takes place, the island of Ireland had been officially divided into the Irish Free State (now known as the Republic of Ireland) and Northern Ireland (still part of the United Kingdom).

Plenty of fictional books, movies, and television shows have used this as a backdrop for intrigue in England proper. (See Season One of Peaky Blinders for an excellent example.) I, too, used the shifting alliances as rationale for why a for-hire spy might conduct an operation in the English countryside.

My story is very much a work of fiction. Count Vasile Zugravescu, the Murphys, Lamberts, Sir Elmer, and Miss Dixon exist only within the confines of my imagination and these pages.

If you'd like to learn more about Irish history, and this particular chapter, I found The Irish Story website to be helpful. (https://www.theirishstory.com/2012/09/18/the-irish-war-of-independence-a-brief-overview/)

On a lighter note, I thoroughly enjoyed learning more about 1920s country house parties and the people who attended them. For months I've been toting an actual paperback copy of Pamela Horn's *Country House Society: The private lives of England's upper class after the First World War* (Amberley Publishing, 2015). The title caught my eye during a visit to Blackwells Bookshop in Oxford, UK. My copy is by now well-worn and filled with page markers, handwritten notes, and underlined passages.

Before I wrap up the historical notes section, I find myself with the unusual circumstances of needing to include a futuristic note. If you've read my Oxford Key cozy mystery series, some aspects of Ducklington Manor might have struck you as familiar. That's because I used it as the setting for Homicide at Holly Manor. I needed a venue where modern-day sleuth Natalie 'Nat' Payne and ghostly versions of Dora and Rex could cross paths. Thus, Ducklington Manor / Holly Manor was born. If you are interested in modern mysteries with a hint of history and a flair of magic, check out my Oxford Key series.

Double Cross Dead
A Dora and Rex 1920s Mystery

An enemy lurks in the prince's inner circle. He'll do anything to escape justice... even commit murder.

England, 1923. Love is in the air and all eyes are on Windsor Castle, where the royal family is celebrating a new royal engagement.

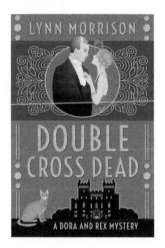

When party invitations are sent to only an elite few, Dora and Rex's invite comes with strings attached.

There's a traitor hiding within the prince's inner circle. Dora and Rex, England's preeminent undercover spy team, are assigned to uncover the turncoat.

Their sole lead is a tip from an anonymous informant. To get the clue, they must meet him privately during the engagement bash.

Lynn Morrison

But, when they show up at the secret rendezvous, instead of a clue, they find a dead body and Rex's best friend Clark holding the murder weapon.

Has Clark turned traitor or was he framed? Can Dora and Rex work double-time to clear their friend's name and identify the real killer before Scotland Yard's leading investigator puts Clark away for life?

Find out in Autumn 2023! Order your copy of Double Cross Dead now on Amazon.

Acknowledgments

I have said many times that writing a book takes a village of support. This one was no exception.

Many thanks to Ken Morrison for reading and giving feedback, one chapter at a time. Thanks also to my Cool Cozy Gang for jumping on a Zoom call when I got stuck in my subplot. You all are amazing.

The writing community keeps me sane. I want to give a special shout-out to Kelly Curtis, Anne Radcliffe, my writing sprint pals, and the FAKAs (you know who you are).

Thanks to Brenda Chapman, Ewa Bartnik, and Fiona Birchall for beta reading the book and providing feedback to make it even better.

As always, Donna L Rogers keeps providing me with phenomenal covers for this series.

To the rest of my friends and family - thanks for being patient with me over the past few months. I'd say life will get easier, but I think we all know I'm lying. Blame the creative muse!

About the Author

Lynn Morrison lives in Oxford, England along with her husband, two daughters and two cats. Born and raised in Mississippi, her wanderlust attitude has led her to live in California, Italy, France, the UK, and the Netherlands. Despite having rubbed shoulders with presidential candidates and members of parliament, night-clubbed in Geneva and Prague, explored Japanese temples and scrambled through Roman ruins, Lynn's real life adventures can't compete with the stories in her mind.

She is as passionate about reading as she is writing, and can almost always be found with a book in hand. You can find out more about her on her website LynnMorrisonWriter.com.

You can chat with her directly in her Facebook group - Lynn Morrison's Not a Book Club - where she talks about books, life and anything else that crosses her mind.

facebook.com/nomadmomdiary

instagram.com/nomadmomdiary

bookbub.com/authors/lynn-morrison

goodreads.com/nomadmomdiary

amazon.com/Lynn-Morrison/e/BooIKC1LVW